THE CUT-THROAT CAFE

NICKI THORNTON

2 PALMER STREET, FROME, SOMERSET BA11 1DS

Text © Nicki Thornton 2020
Illustrations © Matt Saunders 2020

First published in Great Britain in 2020
Chicken House
2 Palmer Street
Frome, Somerset BA11 1DS
United Kingdom
www.chickenhousebooks.com

Cover and interior design by Steve Wells
Cover and inside illustrations by Matt Saunders
Typeset by Dorchester Typesetting Group Ltd
Printed and bound in Great Britain by CPI Group (UK) Ltd, Croydon CR0 4YY

The paper used in this Chicken House book is made from
wood grown in sustainable forests.

1 3 5 7 9 10 8 6 4 2

British Library Cataloguing in Publication data available.

PB ISBN 978-1-912626-60-1
eISBN 978-1-913322-08-3

For my sisters,
Karen and Sandra

Those Appearing in the Curious
Case of the Cut-Throat Cafe

Seth Seppi
Inspector Sagacious Pewter
Angelique Squerr
Nightshade

Herb Camphor
Cheery Damson
Leaf Falling
Dagger Tourmaline
Tendril Vetch

Calamus
Granny Onabutter
Armory Opal
Kalinder Squerr
Gladys Tidings
Forever Young

PART ONE

1. SCRUMDIDDLYUMPTIOUS

'Y ou are to do two things, and two things only.'
Angelique Squerr tossed her long hair, dark
except for a stripe of red down one side. 'You sit
inside this cafe and you wait for me to come back.
You do not cause any trouble.'

Seth Seppi knew that when a magical friend gave
you instructions you should always pay attention.
But he was entranced by the yellow umbrellas
sprouting from circular tables that spilt out in front
of the Scrumdiddlyumptious Cafe. Their fluttering

made it look as if a cloud of giant butterflies had landed in this corner of The Forum, a rather grimy and gloomy cobbled square in the centre of this interesting town.

Angelique tucked her red lacquered cane – a silver-topped magical instrument that she was never without – under her arm and looked ready to go. As she turned and sailed off to do something important, Seth was left with nothing but a heavy suitcase, a cumbersome basket and a feeling that he never did anything right.

Even so, as he lifted the basket and dragged his suitcase awkwardly through the noisily flapping umbrellas, he felt excited.

A smell of warm sugar and cinnamon filled the cold air. He passed only one customer braving the chill outside. A girl with a halo of untidy hair was sitting alone, slumped against the cafe window, her mouth open. She looked as if she'd nodded off halfway through eating a quite delicious-looking strawberry cupcake.

As he stepped inside, a rush of warm air welcomed Seth, along with a woman in a candy-striped dress, her hair in tiny plaits, arranging cakes behind the counter. She greeted Seth with a big, lipsticked smile. Seth smiled back shyly then made his way to an empty seat near the back, but with a clear view of the window. He'd watch for Angelique. She'd hinted that even sitting here and waiting was something he could mess up. Well, he could wait. And he would prove he could steer clear of trouble.

After all, in this friendly cafe, with its walls painted a warm yellow that gave the feeling of being inside a cake or a bowl of custard, what could possibly go wrong?

He tried to position the large basket comfortably on his legs. He reached for a menu, even though today, Seth was less interested in food than looking about him.

Around him were about ten customers munching thick sandwiches, nibbling lunchtime sticky buns or slurping strange-looking foamy green drinks through striped paper straws. There was a comforting low hum of chatter and clink of teaspoons on china, and the smell of toasting cheese.

Seth found himself wondering: *Which of them?*

Because some of these people, reading books or filling in the crossword while they munched, had a secret. A secret that made this cafe the most exciting place he had been to in his life. Some of them were something Seth longed to be more than anything.

Some of them were sorcerers.

'So is this where I get out?' came a soft, lilting voice that didn't disguise its grumpiness. 'It's not dignified being carried around in a basket. Hope you don't expect me to like it. What are we doing here again?'

Not for the first time, Seth wondered whether it really had been a blessing to discover his cat could speak.

There was a girl at a table in the window who had hair as springy and green as moss, and Seth felt that with his slim frame, untidy hair and wide-set eyes, he was unremarkable enough to be able to sit here all day and just watch.

'Nightshade,' he replied softly, 'we are waiting and we are blending in.'

He looked about him. Could he tell if someone was magical?

What about the dapper man in the pinstriped suit at the next table? His gold-patterned waistcoat was straining over his tummy, and two tufts of grey hair sprouted either side of his head as if a bat had landed there badly. The man licked his fingers after making quick work of a crusty sandwich crammed with slices of salami and cheese and went to pay at the till.

'Scrumdiddlyumptious Cafe,' Nightshade muttered. 'Not at all Scrumdiddlyumptious in here. All right for you. I bet you're just about to order something filling and smothered in sugar. Any chance of an ice cream?'

'If a crowd gathers because I've brought a talking cat to this cafe, Angelique will be mad,' Seth whispered into the basket. 'We're in Gramichee, one of the few towns where a cluster of magical folk live.' He repeated Angelique's words from when she explained everything to him earlier, 'But it's not a totally magical town. Sorcerers still have to be secretive.'

Imagine a place where people could walk down the street magicking mice out of fresh air, turning the walls to gold or making it rain fish. But then, Seth knew enough about sorcerers to understand that wasn't ever likely. Sorcerers took their magic seriously. Magic, as well as being incredibly rare, could be dangerous to do.

Seth couldn't stop a small sigh escaping him. Not long ago, he'd started to believe his destiny was to become a sorcerer. But right now he'd settle for being able to use magic to stir a spoon in his tea. Or to perform *any* spell well enough not to cause an explosion.

'So can you please just not talk?' he pleaded to his cat. 'They may even have a *no cats* rule.'

'Well, that's just blatant discrimination. Plenty of places welcome dogs, *adore* dogs, put down nice bowls of fresh water for dogs. Big mucky creatures. You never need to give a cat a bath, do you? You'd think we never came into cafes. Anyway, remind me, how is this all going to help with your magic?'

Seth put his mouth close to the basket. 'Angelique thought it might be good for me to spend some time among magical folk.' Although he suspected what she really meant was that *she* needed some help with him and his disaster magic.

The one thing Seth wanted most in his life, what he dreamt and longed for (apart from, right now, to taste one of those fascinating frothy green drinks), was to be an amazingly powerful sorcerer. The horrible truth beginning to dawn was that this cherished dream might never be realized. Every single time he tried to get a spell under control, it went spectacularly and despairingly wrong.

Angelique had effortlessly summoned a minuscule glow of magical fire in the palm of her hand. On his turn, he'd scorched himself so badly he hadn't been able to practise for days because of the enormous bandage wrapping his hand.

His chance of ever passing the magical exam, the Prospect, and becoming an official member of the magical world, seemed about as likely as flying to the moon.

Worse, he couldn't fight the growing suspicion that if he had inherited even a little of his mother's magic, there was something wrong with it. He stared despondently out of the window, where a boy about thirteen with close-cropped curly black hair and skin the colour of walnuts was threading his way through the yellow umbrellas. He paused by the sleeping girl before pushing open the cafe door, admitting a rush of eager spring air. He slid into a seat, combing the room with anxious eyes.

'Hello, Tendril – hot chocolate?' In one effortless movement the woman at the counter grabbed a wide-rimmed cup and pressed a button that filled the air with the sound of boiling milk.

'Thanks, Glad,' replied the boy.

The tiny girl with hair like moss leapt up. 'Hey, Tendril!' The crafty look on her face and the way she moved to the seat right next to his looked less like friendliness and more like a deliberate attempt to cut off any chance of escape.

The door opened again and in strode an older-looking boy with smooth, raven-black hair and dark eyes as unreflecting as jet. He was wearing a black cape swept about him as if he wanted people to think he had leathery wings.

'Usual please, Glad,' he drawled, tapping his fingers on the counter.

'Trickerchockerglory coming right away, Dagger,' Glad replied, tossing her plaited hair. 'Heard you made your first arrest. I'm impressed!'

Dagger jerked his collar up with a self-satisfied smile. He looked as if he was about to answer, then his hard eyes glittered as he spied the boy called Tendril. A look of fear crossed Tendril's face and he pulled up the hood of his jacket. Dagger took the seat opposite him and the girl with green springy hair giggled unkindly.

Glad went to stand right by their table and planted her hands on her wide hips. 'Just to say, if you apprentices are planning to play any pranks on each other, keep them out of my cafe. Otherwise you'll all be banned. Using spells to give people rabbit ears and turn others blue!' She shook her head as she went back behind the counter.

Apprentices. Seth caught right on to that word.

That meant they must all be training to be magical! Seth looked at the group with curiosity and envy. Apprenticeships were highly prized and were the very best way to learn magic, although using magic to give people rabbit ears and turning others blue really didn't sound like spells that should ever be used.

Glad slid Dagger a giant ice cream in a tall glass, topped with foaming cream and chocolate sprinkles. He shrugged and loaded a spoon.

Even with his imposing air, the enthusiastic way he tucked into his ice cream suggested to Seth he might not be much older than Tendril.

'No more pranks? Aww, shame.' The girl with the green hair gave a sly look at Glad. 'Not here in the Scrum anyway!' Then she jerked down the hood of Tendril's jacket. 'Aww, you got rid of them. Your rabbit ears were so cute.'

Tendril fought to cover his head again and was trying to quickly drain his drink, but it was clearly hot.

Seth hated the way the girl squealed with cruel laughter. He found he was gripping the menu tightly, unable to take his eyes from the group.

Dagger leant towards Tendril. 'I didn't hear you say hello. You should be more polite to your friends.'

'Hello, Dagger,' muttered the boy. It was obvious he was desperate to escape, but was surrounded.

'Did you stop to have a quick chat with Myrtle? Only I notice she's gone to sleep,' Dagger said with a smirk.

There was another snort of laughter from the moss-haired girl.

Tendril began to sneeze. His breathing quickly became fast and shallow and soon he was fighting to get air into his lungs. His eyes were watering. He fumbled to reach his pocket.

Seth was almost on his feet, but then Glad was there and reaching into Tendril's pocket for him. She drew out a slender square-cut green bottle. He nodded, eyes watering, breathing raspy. Glad unscrewed the lid, sprinkled a few drops into a glass of water and handed it to the choking boy. He took a gulp and his sneezing immediately subsided, then he was breathing normally again.

'Did someone just give him something?' snapped Glad. 'If this is another prank, you'll all be banned. I mean it.'

No one said anything and Glad stomped off to clear the table outside, her angry steps echoing the furious beating of Seth's heart. And then, without warning, the menu Seth was clutching became a jet of flame that roared upwards. He shoved the burning menu into a jug of water and leapt to his feet, sending Nightshade's basket toppling to the floor. He glanced around, hoping for once he'd been lucky and put out the flare before anyone had noticed.

There was still a plume of smoke and the smell of scorching.

Seth grabbed the basket and his suitcase and dashed for the door, just as from outside there came a crash of breaking china. For a moment, Seth thought he'd managed to cause that too and almost collided with Glad rushing back in to the cafe. She had both hands clapped to her face below wide, terrified eyes.

On the ground outside, next to the sleeping girl, was a shattered plate and a mess of strawberry cupcake.

'Help!' Glad cried. 'Someone call a doctor! Now! It's Myrtle Rust, she's – she's – Oh my moon and stars! I think she might be dead!'

2. MAGICAL HQ

'**D**id you just start a fire?' came Nightshade's grumpy voice. 'And what was that about someone dying?'

In a terrible panic, Seth raced out past the jumble of circular tables and into the cobbled main square, struggling with his battered suitcase and the basket. He headed in the direction Angelique had taken.

'You've been in Gramichee less than an hour. You've left a blackened, sooty trail and possibly a dead body. Let's hope she's just ill,' said Nightshade.

'Angelique told you to stay out of trouble and wait in the cafe. But as you messed up both of those, I think it was the right move to leave. Must say, those apprentices seemed more cut-throat than scrumdiddlyumptious.'

Seth focused on threading through the twisting, narrow streets. He stopped and turned once or twice, feeling hopelessly lost and as if the streets were closing in and becoming narrower after he'd passed through.

Finally, he located a tiny side road, facing an insignificant shop in dark blue that blended into the buildings either side so well you had to look at it several times to check it was really there.

'Main Street, number thirty-six,' he muttered doubtfully 'This is supposed to be the Elysee, the headquarters of the organization that runs the magical world. It can't be the right place.' He squinted through dark windows. 'All I can see are colourful jars of sweets.'

'What were you expecting – a moving castle, or maybe a big sign saying *get your magic potions here*?' said Nightshade. 'As you just said, everyone still has to keep it a secret that there's magic here. It's hardly going to advertise that everyone working here is magical. It'll just be a cover.'

Annoyingly, Nightshade had a point. She had a habit of seeing things before Seth did. 'Angelique's here at a meeting.' Seth sat down on his suitcase. 'I'll just wait.'

Angelique was only a couple of years older than Seth, but she was an agent for an Elysee department called Sinister Speculation Services, or S3 for short. She possessed extraordinarily strong natural magic and went undercover into places that might be contaminated by remains of magic. Her job was to make things safe. It was secretive and dangerous work. She called it 'cleaning'.

'You might like being out here in this wind, but it's whistling right through this basket. Are you going to let me out of this thing?' asked Nightshade. 'When you said we were going on our travels, I didn't know you meant to keep me locked up. And I'm going to need a wee soon.'

Before Seth could reply, a figure rushed through the door of the old-fashioned sweet shop and almost cannoned into him. He started to apologize before recognizing the tall man – he looked different today, in a sober navy suit, a pale blue shirt and a dark, narrow tie, but there was no denying who it was . . .

'Inspector Pewter!' cried Seth.

Pewter's silver hair had received the attention of a

very efficient barber. It was short, neat and shaved at the sides and looked as recently polished as his very shiny shoes.

'Seth!' The tall figure stopped. 'Glad to see you, but I'm just on my way to sort out a little trouble with the apprentices.'

By 'a little trouble', Seth hazarded a guess the inspector might be on his way to the body at the Scrumdiddlyumptious, and he had no intention of mentioning he'd just come from there himself. He'd sincerely meant to follow Angelique's instructions and steer well clear of the merest hint of trouble.

'Is this a big day for us both?' Pewter turned to push open the door he'd raced through and held it wide to let Seth past with his basket and suitcase. 'Not every day I get a new boss, and . . . you can't be here for your Prospect already?'

'New boss? Thought you were looking smart.' Seth couldn't help but grin as he bundled in his suitcase and the basket. He avoided that question about his Prospect.

He had begun to allow himself to dream that one day he might even become a magical detective, like Pewter, and work for MagiCon, investigating magical crime. But right now his ambition went no further than wanting to perform a simple spell and not blow everything up.

'Am I really allowed in? I'm just waiting for Angelique.'

'Not if you've got a dangerous animal in that basket.'

'It's not a dangerous animal, it's Nightshade.'

'Exactly what I thought.'

Pewter didn't object when Seth stepped inside and looked around. He'd guessed Nightshade would be right when she'd said that the shop was just a front, a magical screen to protect Elysee HQ from curious outsiders, but the room was simply full of colourful jars – with labels like RHUBARB AND CUSTARD or BARLEY TWISTS – stretching up to the ceiling. There were also shelves of stacked candles in every size and colour, some in the moulded shapes of animals, or conical with stripes with even more exotic names and scents than the sweets. VIOLET TROPICAL STORM, ICED MANGO DELIGHT, ESPECIALLY SALTY SEA SPRAY.

Such a bewildering mix of colours and smells would be a nightmare for anyone who had trouble making choices. Seth waited for Pewter to open some sort of secret entrance, or maybe a trapdoor. Anything felt possible. A portal into another world?

Pewter lifted the lid on a jar of treacle toffee.

'Are you nervous about having a new boss?' Seth asked.

'Nervous? Not in the slightest.' Pewter fumbled putting the lid back on and little sweets scattered across the floor. They started to wriggle into brown, wormlike shapes. 'Perhaps a little. Doesn't help that I've just had to deposit a rock band in the evidence room and I couldn't stop it singing. Nothing I ever do leads to a promotion.' He sighed and started sucking on a toffee. He offered a small bowl of sweets to Seth.

'You locked a band in the evidence room?'

'A *rock* band.' The inspector spoke with difficulty through his toffee. 'A group of rocks that have been charmed to sing.'

'What's your new boss like?' Seth asked, popping a lurid green sweet into his mouth.

'I have learnt one important fact that means we will get along famously,' said Pewter. 'I'll be working for someone who was an incredible tennis player in their youth.' Every moment of his free time, Pewter loved to play tennis.

As Seth sucked on the sweet, he saw a worried look crossing Inspector Pewter's face. Together they had faced murderers, battled dangerous sinister magic, dodged ice spears and escaped entire cliffs raining down on them – and the inspector had always looked unruffled, as if it was all in a day's work. This was the first time Seth had seen him look uneasy.

The sweet exploded in Seth's mouth with a piercing flavour that felt as if his cheeks were being sucked down his throat. He began to cough, his eyes watering so much he could only dimly make out Pewter taking a *strawberry sunrise* candle. He lit it and the air was immediately filled with the sweet smell of ripe summer fruit.

Seth was fighting not to spit out the sharp sweet. Through his watering eyes and coughing, he waved away smoke, keen to follow Pewter's example. He fumbled with a match to light the nearest candle – *spiced peach*. The flame caught and the air filled with pungent spices so heavy Seth only spluttered more.

Then both candles were extinguished at once, leaving them in a smoky darkness. The wall beyond the counter at the back of the shop dissolved. Or Seth thought it did. He was having difficulty seeing through the smoke.

Pewter gestured as a drab-looking corridor appeared. It was painted a vile green, dotted with countless doors and seemingly without end. Seth tried to dry his eyes, because he realized this was it.

The hub of the magical world.

'Welcome to the Factory,' said Pewter. 'At least that's what we call it. Don't quite know how it got that name, seeing as we don't make anything, except for a lot of hot air and a surprisingly large amount of paperwork.'

Seth hadn't known what to expect. As they set off down the corridor, Seth peered through any open door they passed. In every one, people were rushing about waving sheaves of paper and moving boxes. No one appeared to be doing anything magical. A short man in a checked suit raced past carrying an evil-looking toy rabbit sealed inside a plastic evidence bag.

Pewter looked at Seth through his little round glasses. 'Now, I really should get back to my troublesome apprentices.' He pointed along the endless corridor. 'You'll find Angelique behind the last door.'

As Seth headed further and further down the corridor, the bustle and chatter started to fade, until all he could hear was his boots squeaking on the vinyl floor. Then the vinyl was replaced by a soft carpet. And then there was only one closed door ahead, with two metal cabinets next to it.

'Are we in the right place?' came Nightshade's

voice from the depths of the basket. 'How about you open the door just a smidge and check.'

Seth hesitated. Being caught eavesdropping on an important meeting was not a smart move. He turned the handle very slowly and pushed the heavy door open just the tiniest crack.

Then he caught Angelique's voice. 'The trouble is, he really needs a *lot* of help with his magic.'

Seth froze. It sounded like this important meeting was about him.

3. MAGIC OF A STRANGE, EXPLOSIVE KIND

Seth squeezed himself in between the two big metal cabinets outside the door. He pulled Nightshade's basket awkwardly in after him. He had to listen, because Angelique's dejected tone made Seth's stomach feel as if it was trying to freefall to his shoes.

A woman's voice replied. Smooth, like skates on ice. 'Someone with dangerously explosive magic and a disturbingly steep learning curve ahead of him. Not the best use of your time.'

'He's a friend. I can't let him down.'

It *was* about him. Seth spoke in a low voice to Nightshade. 'She's getting into trouble over me.'

'She's your friend! Of course she wants to help you.'

The smooth voice was carrying on. 'I know you don't like to take advice from people only trying to help you, but it's time someone pointed out that there are those better qualified to bring him up to Prospect standards. Have you tried to find him a principal and a proper apprenticeship?'

Seth longed to be offered an apprenticeship. But first, Angelique had taken on the tricky challenge of trying to teach him enough magic so he could get through his Prospect safely – this was where you got a chance to prove you had a spark of magic. If he didn't blow up anything and passed, he would be invited to be part of the magical world and be awarded an Elysee library card and gain access to all the magical texts. It was the way sorcerers could study to improve their magic.

If he was supremely lucky, he might find himself an apprenticeship and study with a principal. But apprenticeships, particularly those with the best principals, were highly prized and much fought over.

'He may do something brilliant. But his magic

is . . . I can't see anyone taking him on,' admitted Angelique.

There was a short pause before the glacial tones were heard again. 'Have you actually asked yourself if teaching him magic is even a good idea?' There came an irritated tapping sound; it sounded like a pencil was being taught a lesson. 'What if he does real harm? You can't afford to feel responsible. His mother—'

'Seth's not like that!' interrupted Angelique. 'It's just that his magic is of a strange, explosive kind.'

The fact that Seth came from a magical family was something he had only learnt recently, when Angelique had arrived at Seth's home, the Last Chance Hotel.

Seth was desperate to prove that he did possess that much-prized spark of true magic. But he had also learnt that his mother was accused of being on the wrong side of sorcery – the sinister side, the side that used magic to hurt people, wield power and do bad things.

He was already facing the fact that learning magic would be no easy path.

Hearing doubts about his mother expressed in that smooth, commanding voice made Seth ask himself, not for the first time – *should* he even be learning magic? What if the only magical talent he possessed was to perform magic on the sinister side? Was that the reason behind his continual failure to master decent, well-intentioned magic?

What if he was dangerous?

The icy voice was continuing. 'You've turned down the last two cases assigned to you. To neglect your own responsibilities for someone who might prove unsuitable . . .'

Seth was shocked. He'd never thought to ask how Angelique was finding the time to help him. She had an important and serious career. She helped rid the world of all sorts of dangerous magic. Seth had seen her battling with more frightening things than most people even knew existed.

If she had been neglecting that to help him, then the world was not as protected as it needed to be, and it was his fault.

He heard Angelique being asked another devastatingly poignant question. 'If he's a friend, why is he letting you jeopardize your career?'

'I can learn magic by myself,' he muttered to Nightshade as the truth sank in.

Why had he been so selfish to never even question if she had the time to help him? He had to put this right. He had to go home to the Last Chance Hotel and stop bothering Angelique.

But first, he had to unwedge himself from between the two filing cabinets.

Between him, his suitcase and Nightshade's basket, he couldn't even get out of this corridor. He was forced to listen to even more uncomfortable truths as he tried to wrench himself free.

'Unpredictable and explosive is not an easy combination to sell to a principal. Overcoming such a well-known – let's be frank – notorious mother presents interesting challenges too. Luckily, I am not without influence. You have done more than enough, my dear girl. Let's take this troublesome boy off your hands. It's time to say goodbye.'

Angelique had gone quiet.

'Someone's coming towards the door,' hissed Nightshade. But her basket was completely wedged. Seth desperately tried to haul it free.

'Let him have his chance with the Prospect.' The glacial voice was edging closer. 'The Elysee will decide if he has the requisite spark of magic. We shall set his Prospect for a month's time.'

At the exact moment Seth made a final frantic effort and exploded like a cork out of a champagne bottle, the door opened. He landed on his knees, level with high-heeled boots. Looking up, he saw a tall, elegant woman, dark hair presented in an elaborate knot on her head. She had beautiful, slanting, almond-coloured eyes and was dressed in a dove-grey suit.

She looked at Seth coolly. It must have been pretty obvious the boy with the untidy hair, bright-blue tunic and oversized cat basket had been listening outside her door.

A hand was extended towards Seth, one with long fingernails painted a shimmering midnight blue. Seth looked up at those almond-coloured eyes, hauled himself upright and took the hand of the most impressively glamorous woman he'd ever met. He was aware Angelique had her furious face on.

'Seth Seppi? I've heard so much about you.'

Seth blushed – and everything she'd heard had been bad.

The office behind her had floor-to-ceiling windows with views out on to a cool sea of floating ice floes and a flinty-blue sky. There was even a fresh tang of salt in the air. It was as if someone had magically deposited an oasis of cool, calm quiet at the end of the bustling building.

Angelique stepped forward. 'Seth, this is the new head of MagiCon.'

This was Pewter's new boss? No wonder the

inspector was nervous.

Seth knew he shouldn't really stare, but he'd noticed that in among her long hair, twisted into submission, he could just make out one stripe of red, exactly the same as Angelique's.

'Kalinder Squerr.' Seth's hand was released, and the glamorous woman turned her penetrating gaze to Angelique with just the hint of a smile. 'And would it completely kill you to call me *Mother*?'

4. KALINDER SQUERR

'You heard all of that, didn't you?' Angelique stomped ahead, while Seth scampered after, struggling with his suitcase and the cat basket.

'Some of it, maybe.'

'I won't ask how staying in the Scrum and keeping out of trouble could possibly have been interpreted as coming and listening in on a meeting between me and the new head of MagiCon.'

'That was your mother! She's pretty impressive,' said Seth as they swept through the sweetly scented candle and sweet shop and out into Main Street. High above, the tall spire of a nearby church could be seen piercing the fierce cloudless blue of the sky.

Angelique turned, saw Seth struggling with his suitcase and took it from him. 'At least it'll save me telling you the good news.'

What, that your mother has pulled strings just to find someone to take me off your hands, because I'm too dangerous to be around?

What didn't he know about Angelique? What had it been like growing up with a mother who looked like she'd give you six impossible challenges before breakfast? He'd always been curious about how she had ended up with such a tough job so young. There were things about Angelique he guessed he never would know.

Angelique said nothing as she led the way back through the narrow, twisting streets, and Seth thought his friend's only wish was to be rid of him as quickly as possible.

He understood vaguely that he was to be given the chance of an apprenticeship. But how was that possible? Magical training had long been the privilege of those from old, illustrious sorcerer families. Or had been, until a brave and controversial new policy actively sought out those with magical talent instead of safeguarding the cream of apprenticeships for the oldest families.

Because the truth was that magic was not always passed on in families. Anyone might be born with a spark of magic. Years of not seeking out magic wherever it might be found had led to the magical world being in crisis.

Magic was dying out.

They turned a couple of times more and were back on the edge of the cobbled square. The Forum was surrounded by ancient buildings that sleepily leant on each other for support. Some were white-painted with sagging timbers and tiny windows, but some were startlingly modern, as if the whole lot had been shuffled and put back together randomly.

As Seth hurtled after Angelique, he was longing to explore. He spied a sandwich shop squeezed in next to a chemist and a tiny bookshop nestled on one side of the Scrum. On the other was a shopfront painted black, the word *Darkheart* written in gothic lettering above gloomy windows. *Which of them?* He asked himself the question again. *How could you tell which were magical businesses?*

The cafe looked closed. Seth darted a guilty glance towards it and thought any MagiCon detectives must have gone efficiently about their work as there were no signs of any activity beyond the noisy flapping of the yellow umbrellas.

He scurried after Angelique, sticking close to her as he fought a rising panic that what Mrs Squerr had planned for him was going to be a disaster. He'd never be ready to take his Prospect in a month.

Then they stopped outside a shabby and unloved shop with peeling paint the rich green of beech leaves. There was a single window that hadn't been washed in a long time. It was a tiny shop in the middle of a small town, yet Seth's nose was telling him of damp places, swamps, the familiar whiff of forests and their carpet of a mulch of fallen leaves. It reminded him so much of his ramshackle hotel, miles away in the middle of the dense, never-ending Last Hope Forest, left behind in a rush of excitement. Now all he felt was a tighter knot of fear. How long would he be away?

Above the shop door, in very faded gold lettering, was the word *Curorium*. That also was familiar. Ethylene Despair, head librarian of the Elysee library of magical books, had given him *Curology: Herbal Essences and Their Magical Uses* when he'd once sneaked into the library, telling him it would suit him. He'd looked through it eagerly and suggested Angelique help him try some of the magic from the book, but she had just wrinkled her nose. 'A curo-mage, or curologist, is incredibly rare,' she'd said. 'It's a very precise and specialist form of magic. Reme-dies. Potions. I think someone would have to eat or drink them, Seth, to see if you'd done them properly.' She had pushed the book back.

'And you're not experimenting on me,' Nightshade had put in helpfully and quickly. 'Although there are a few spare crows about that nobody would miss.'

Seth had known enough about his magic to accept how terrible he'd feel if even one crow exploded horribly because of him, and the conversa-tion had ended there.

But he'd brought the book with him in his battered suitcase, and he had a small hope that maybe someone here might teach him how to use it.

Angelique squared her shoulders and announced, 'This is it!' And then headed for the shop next door.

Seth had hardly given that one a glance. It was a bright pillar-box red with paint so new Seth couldn't resist touching it to see if it was still wet. The window was crammed full of strange and colourful objects.

'Any time is great to let me out, Seth,' muttered Nightshade from the basket. 'Sitting in that cafe was torture. Just a drink or a snack any time this afternoon would have been nice. And I *really* do need a wee now.'

Seth bent to unclip the front and watched his slinky black cat bound out and disappear into a narrow passage between the two shops. He straightened his tunic and finger-combed his untidy hair and readied himself to follow Angelique inside, unsure what awaited him.

Opening the door set off a sweet tinkling, like a chandelier brushed by a breeze. Feathery dreamcatchers, healing crystals, wind chimes and tiny charms dangled from the ceiling and swung together in a joyful dance. The air was sweet with gingerbread and vanilla, a hint of rose petals and sugar mice. And something Seth couldn't quite place. It made him stop and take deep breaths to try to identify it. Maybe garlic? Maybe limeflower?

Angelique threw him a fierce look that told him to stop sniffing.

'We're here to see Forever Young,' she announced to a girl with a thick wedge of aubergine-coloured hair and big boots the same colour who was standing sullenly behind the counter.

The girl unfolded her arms and with slow reluctance disappeared through a rear door.

Angelique paused by a basket of amber bottles on

cords: AMULETS – PROTECT YOUR LOVED ONES AND SURVIVE. Her lip curled in distaste and she wrinkled her nose in the direction of a wall crammed with shelves of different coloured rocks and crystals, all shouting with claims of amazing magical properties, from healing joint pain to curing an aching heart.

Seth picked up a soft, pale worm-like object with a label attached: WIGGLE AWAY YOUR WORRIES – TELL YOUR WIGGLE YOUR WORRIES AND THEY WILL DISAPPEAR! Maybe he should buy a dozen – if they actually worked. They didn't exactly look magical.

A petite woman arrived from the back of the shop, her arms spread wide. She was dressed in an elaborate full-length embroidered green skirt threaded with tiny mirrors so that she scattered little shivers of light as she walked. She had extravagantly long auburn hair and a beaming smile. The smell of rose petals got stronger as she approached.

'Welcome! Forever Young at your service. How can we help you lovely people?' She saw Angelique holding an amulet. 'Oh, you have chosen well, those are *wonderful*. And on special offer – you can buy ten for the price of eight.'

Angelique dropped the amber amulet back into the basket. 'We are here because I think you might be able to act as principal to my friend here?'

Angelique nodded at Seth, who tried to look confident, but felt his hair being stroked with a long pink feather dangling from the ceiling. That and the overpowering scent of rosewater made him fight not to sneeze.

It was the girl with the aubergine hair who spoke up. 'I think you'll find Miss Young already has an apprentice – that would be me, Cheery Damson.' She was smiling, with bared teeth telling Seth she'd eat him rather than share an apprenticeship.

Seth wished he could disappear through the floor. Angelique handed over a folded piece of paper. 'Er – my mother . . .'

Miss Young read the note quickly, her face changing and her eyes flickering to the distinctive stripe of red in Angelique's glossy dark hair.

'Well, how absolutely kind of Mrs Squerr to take an interest in my little business,' she tinkled, a pale hand flapping at her throat as she looked nervously at Cheery Damson.

Cheery glared under her heavy purple fringe as if Seth was something she'd just found on the sole of her matching boot.

Nightshade had slipped in behind them and Seth waited, in horror, for her to speak and really add to the awkwardness.

But something even worse happened.

Nightshade pounced, a fraction of a second after Seth had caught sight of a flash of fur and a tail as a brown mouse made a run across the floor. Everyone was transfixed by Nightshade killing her prey. She looked up into the difficult silence, a little body dangling limply from her mouth. She was completely unabashed by having committed murder in front of them and her expression seemed to say *what?*, and maybe *lunch*.

Miss Young moved forwards and Seth was convinced that they were getting thrown out. But she clasped her hands together. 'Oh, how clever! You are so much better than Gorgeous Tom at catching things and this shop does seem a teensy bit overrun. We've only been open such a short time and I never imagined we were going to have quite so many little friends.'

She moved towards Seth and he found himself enveloped in a soft rose-petals hug. 'Seth Seppi, you have brought me a solution to our little – ahem – problem. Welcome. Welcome to the Belle Boutique. And congratulations! You've got yourself a month's trial for an apprenticeship! Your future starts here. As long as your *beautiful* cat stays with you. Deal?'

5. WE'LL BE SO COSY

Miss Young led the way past a small but extremely untidy kitchen, waving at it vaguely and saying that was where they mixed up everything, and into a short, dark corridor. She threw open a door and Seth was staring at a storeroom crammed with huge plastic tubs and a lot of small, white cardboard boxes stamped with colourful labels. Pick-me-up Peppermints – perfect when flagging in the middle of the afternoon; Delicious Demise – instant death to defects.

'I'm on the top floor,' Miss Young twittered, tossing back her cascade of shining auburn hair and heading into the depths to rummage, bringing forth a grimy holdall that looked like she might have had it since her school days. 'I just love to look out at the moon and stars. Cheery's on the first floor.'

Seth concentrated on avoiding Cheery's stare, hostile as a security guard who had discovered him breaking in. But Cheery loomed in threateningly close.

'I have first dibs on the bathroom in the morning,' she breathed, as if trying to scorch him like a dragon. 'And any food in the fridge.'

Miss Young scraped off sticky grey cobwebs from the holdall, reached in and chucked aside a dented tin water bottle and a hockey stick stamped with a worn school crest, and finally extracted a moth-eaten and almost definitely mice-chewed hammock.

It was only as she strung the hammock between a couple of pipes and tested it for strength that the truth dawned: this was to be his room for the next month.

There was a regular humming noise and it was sweatily hot, leading Seth to guess the storeroom was above the boiler. Things were happening too fast, and when he noticed a rear exit he felt he wanted to just carry on through and keep going.

He guessed this was what happened when Kalinder Squerr took charge. He had a month to learn what Miss Young could teach him, so he wouldn't be a waste of anyone else's time. His Prospect would come alarmingly soon. Right now, he thought he had about as much chance of passing it as getting a good night's sleep here.

'Three of us.' Miss Young clapped her hands. 'Four, including your very talented cat. We'll be so cosy.' She giggled down at Nightshade, who looked up, green eyes gleaming.

Seth hoped she hadn't dropped a half-chewed mouse anywhere.

Cosy. If he so much as caused a tiny explosion practising his magic in here, those white boxes were going to go up like a bonfire.

Angelique dropped his battered suitcase alongside the cat basket and told him she'd leave him to settle in, as if she couldn't wait to be rid of him. A few seconds later the tinkling of the front door bell told him she had gone. This was it.

'What's your affinity?' Cheery slouched against the door with her arms crossed as Miss Young shoved aside a couple of the vast plastic tubs. 'Apart from getting in the way?' she muttered low enough so Miss Young wouldn't hear.

Questions about magic were always tricky. There was a huge void in Seth's magical knowledge. Neither of his parents had ever given him the slightest hint of his true history or that he might carry sorcery in his blood. He'd only accidentally learnt of the existence of magic. He really did not want Cheery to know just what a beginner he was.

And what would she think if she found out about his mother? Inspector Pewter had been able to release her from the firefly cage, a dark magical device in which she'd been trapped, but she was now in Ward 23, a hospital for magical folk, in some sort of magically induced coma, waiting to be questioned about her sinister past. If she ever regained consciousness.

Miss Young threw her long curtain of hair over her shoulder, twinkled kindly at Seth and patted Nightshade. 'We'll leave you to settle in. Come through when you're ready. Cheery will show you the rest. No rush.'

Cheery lingered to hiss a warm threatening breath close to his ear. 'No rush.'

As Seth tested the hammock, he reached into a handy inside pocket of the bright-blue tunic he wore and took out a small black book. It was so old, with pages held together with a scarlet thread. It was full of simple family recipes, mostly. But it was also sprinkled with the odd spell, some banned spells and details of dark devices and sinister ideas. Even as he held it, it felt so right, so comfortable in his hand; it was like being close to a trusted friend. And that was the trouble. It had been his mother's. And for this reason, for the first time since he'd found it, he stopped carrying it with him and tucked it right away in the bottom of his suitcase.

He had cramped and sweaty lodgings. He had Cheery. *But this is still a great opportunity*, he told himself firmly.

He was doing a month's trial as an apprentice. He'd get proper, experienced instruction and find a way to do magic that wasn't dangerously explosive or from sinister sources. He could do this.

All he needed was one spell he could demonstrate impressively enough to pass his Prospect.

He would not let Angelique nor her mother down.

His first introduction to magical training turned out to be Miss Young's twittering insistence about greeting everyone with a smile, although that seemed to be something Cheery hadn't perfected yet. He didn't know how long Cheery had been here.

The most vital tip he picked up was how not to

lose any fingers to a till that snapped aggressively every time he rang up another sale.

Between avoiding catching Cheery's eye as she constantly gave him the evils from under her thick aubergine wedge of hair, and not ending up with fewer fingers, time passed more dangerously than he had anticipated. Finally, Miss Young took him to the kitchen prep room. This was it. The path to magic was to begin.

The small kitchen area was crazily untidy. Seth could recognize a load of washing-up when he saw it, and was dismayed when Miss Young frowned and said: 'Maybe just start with a little tidying.' She then slipped on a full-length black coat and announced she had to go out.

'I'll leave you two to make friends. Cheery Damson, you are in charge! Prices are on the packets. Sell, sell, sell!' She smiled and put a finger alongside her rosebud mouth. 'And please assemble the ingredients for my Fingernails Finest.'

Cheery moved forwards eagerly.

'But no actual mixing.' Miss Young wagged a finger in Cheery's disappointed face. 'Not without me.'

She flipped up the hood of her coat to cover her shining hair, grabbed a bulging black bag with tough metal fasteners and headed for the door. Then she dashed back, took one of the white boxes, ripped it open and stirred a large spoonful of Perfectly Prime Powders into a glass of water. She drank quickly, closing her eyes as she finished the glass. 'Ah!'

She gave a gentle hiccup that she covered with the back of her hand. 'Delicious! And so refreshing. Who was so clever as to invent a lovely restorative medicine that tastes like candyfloss? Oh, that was me,' she said with a tinkly little laugh. 'Now I have a medical emergency. So very tiring being so popular and always in demand.' She swept out, dangling a stethoscope around her neck.

He was alone with Cheery.

'Wow, her magical remedies are very in demand,' said Seth, picking up one of the white boxes of Fingernails Finest from the stack behind the counter. 'Are you learning loads?'

By way of reply, he was grabbed around the neck and tossed into the pile of white boxes. He tried to scrabble to his feet, but Cheery shoved him back again. He tried to push her off and yelled: 'What's up with you?' and finally made it back to his feet. 'What have I done?'

'*What have I done?*' Cheery mimicked in a childish voice. 'What the hairy fishcakes do you even mean by shoving your way in here? Trying to steal my apprenticeship?'

'That's not fair! I'm only here for a month – can't we make the best of it? I'm sure we can work together.' He was completely sure of the opposite.

'So you've no plans to stitch me up so she slings *me* out at the end of the month and keeps you and your blasted murderous cat she's fallen in love with?'

Seth shook his head and straightened his tunic. Now she'd planted the thought, getting rid of Cheery was not entirely a bad idea.

In one swift movement, she grabbed him by the wrist and yanked his arm up and painfully behind him.

'All right, so here's the deal. You do the work. I go to my CWK classes. You say nothing to Miss Young.'

'CWK?' Seth managed, trying not to let on how much Cheery was hurting him.

'Chopping, wrestling and kickboxing. I've got a grading coming and I need to practise on someone. That way I might catch up what I've missed while doing this lousy apprenticeship.' Cheery held her free hand out, inviting Seth to shake.

He would be sleeping in a mouldy old hammock and his fellow apprentice was hurting his arm so much his eyes were watering with the effort of not crying out. But he was going to be learning magic.

He'd always known it would be tough. He needed to pass that Prospect. He had a month. What choice did he have?

Seth winced and with his free hand reached for Cheery's. He shook it.

6. Granny Onabutter's Knitting

'**B**y medical emergency she means someone's eyebrows need trimming. Or a rogue grey hair someone's found before a date,' Cheery rattled out. 'Something truly awful.'

She ducked under a dangle of feathery dream-catchers, hurled herself into a beanbag in a secluded corner behind the counter and rootled through another pile of white boxes before extracting a tatty novel.

Seth eyed the gruesome cover. Hadn't Miss Young

just left instructions to assemble ingredients for Fingernails Finest?

'Customer! All yours!' Cheery buried her nose in her well-thumbed spy novel as, from outside the window, came a slow and ominous *shuffle-shuffle-thud*.

Seth stared at stacks of identical white boxes behind the counter in a panic. 'But I can't tell Delicious Demise from Pick-me-up Peppermints. I have absolutely no idea what I am doing.'

'Same. I've been here a month and all know is that I don't wanna to spend my life recommending healing crystals and foot powder. Unless the foot powder makes you run faster or kick doors down more easily. Yeah, wouldn't be so bad if we were making foot powder that made you run faster. S'what magic should be used for. Anyway, I wouldn't worry, it'll only be Granny Onabutter.'

As the door opened with its delightful chime, Cheery snuggled deep into the beanbag. 'She'll want her Perfectly Prime Powders. But not before a very long, loooong gossip. Want a word of advice?'

Seth looked in distress at the tower of identical white boxes, all with weird names. 'Yes please.'

'Don't get her started on knitting patterns.'

Granny Onabutter could have been aged

anywhere from seventy to over a hundred. She wandered in with a slow shuffle, her back curved in reflection of her elaborate walking stick, which was shaped like an elephant's trunk. She clutched a picnic basket and blinked at Seth, her eyes two dark pips in a face like a dried apple. It made Seth think of currant buns and cooking back in the kitchen of the Last Chance Hotel. She smiled, revealing beautiful even teeth.

'Well, young man, haven't seen you before,' she blinked. 'Just visiting?' Her curranty eyes searched over his shoulder. 'Now I'm not one to gossip, but I presume Miss Young and Cheery have heard about the terrible state of Myrtle Rust?'

Myrtle Rust! That was the name of the girl who had collapsed outside the Scrum. Seth was eager for news – it really sounded as if something serious had happened.

Granny Onabutter lifted the elephant's trunk stick and headed to a red chair shaped like a pair of lips. She jabbed at a hairy orange cushion. With a yowl and a hiss, the cushion unfurled itself. 'Oh my beautiful beast. Gorgeous Tom,' crooned Granny, tickling the cat under the chin, which he clearly didn't like and stalked off, the glossy fur of his tail held high.

Cheery hoisted herself out of the beanbag. 'What's happened to Myrtle?' she demanded, approaching the corner where Granny Onabutter had edged herself on to the red chair and retrieved a half-knitted item in a soft, pink wool from her basket.

'Well, no one from MagiCon would tell me a blinking thing, even though I hung around the Scrum for ages.' Granny Onabutter put on glasses and laboriously looped pink wool around a long metal needle. 'But Myrtle Rust was found in a right deathly slumber sitting outside. People couldn't get out of the cafe fast enough. MagiCon running about, trying to keep things quiet. Was it something she ate, or . . . Dung and goats cheese! Dropped three stitches! Is this a prank gone wrong? A bunch of the apprentices were in the cafe at the time.'

'A prank on Myrtle?' repeated Cheery. 'In the Scrum?' She flew to the window, where you could see the fluttering yellow umbrellas on the opposite side of the square and the frowning window of Dark-heart next door.

Granny fished around in her wicker basket, brought out a second pair of half-moon glasses, swapped them and peered afresh at the square of knitting. 'Don't see as well as I used to. Will have to do this over.' She looked at Cheery over the top of her new glasses. Her needles began to clack. 'It does look like Myrtle Rust has been struck down by some very crafty sinister magic indeed.'

She was not the first person Seth had heard talk about sinister magic with a sort of revered awe.

He had overheard the talk in the Scrum about spells. That girl with the green hair had jerked back Tendril's hood and said something about furry ears, and Glad had mentioned banning 'pranks' rather than anything really dark. Yet it sounded like Myrtle had been hit by magic far more dangerous. Seth found Granny had fixed him with her bright little eyes.

'Are you another apprentice? So glad our very talented Miss Young is passing on all her knowledge. I swear by her powders, haven't felt so sprightly in years. You're going to learn such secrets!'

'I'm just here to help for a month,' he explained as he introduced himself, giving an uneasy glance at Cheery. 'I haven't passed the Prospect, Mrs Onabutter. Cheery and Miss Young are doing me a favour.'

'Oh, I wouldn't worry about the fuddling Prospect,' she tutted at Seth kindly. 'You'll be fine. And just call me Granny. Everyone else does.'

Her metal needles clashed like fencing swords as

she speedily added another row, explaining to Seth how Myrtle was the apprentice of Quartz Dark-heart. 'Supposedly the best scientific inventor of our age. Although Quartz is more of a pedlar of magical artefacts – runs Darkheart.' She pointed with a long knitting needle towards the shop on the opposite side of the square.

'Is that what MagiCon think? That one of the apprentices has gone too far?' quizzed Cheery.

'Our apprentice scheme is doing wonders for the magical community. But you apprentices, you lovely young people, will have your little jokes.' Granny's knitting went back in her lap. 'Putting rabbit ears on poor Tendril . . . not a kind thing to learn to do.' Granny shook her head indulgently. 'Here in Gramichee we attract the best sorcerers. All so competitive. I remember that age. So important to be top hound. But too many clever people in one place . . . it gets a little . . . cut-throat.'

'Seth should watch himself, taking an apprentice-ship in Gramichee right now, shouldn't he, Granny?' said Cheery, who had given up glaring out of the window and had moved behind Seth like an evil pixie waiting to cast a bad spell.

'Oh, I'm sure we needn't panic, not just yet,' said Granny with relish. 'No one wants the apprentice scheme scrapped, not now it's all bubbling along so nicely. But it is a terrible worry that things have *escalated.*'

'The apprentice scheme scrapped?' asked Cheery, disbelieving Granny's doom-laden warning. 'How serious is this attack on Myrtle?'

'I'm sure she'll completely recover. Where there's a pulse there's hope, eh?' Granny's face scrunched like old paper into a smile. 'Just need to get whoever's behind it to own up to what spell was used. Or get all the Elysee's best experts delving into what's cursed her. That's the way! Find the weakness in whatever she's been struck with. Then she might stand a chance of it being unpicked.'

'Why would any of the apprentices play a prank using such serious magic?' Cheery sounded worried and confused. 'The apprentices know they're not allowed to use magic for pranks. Would any of them even know that sort of spell?'

'Now I'm not one to point the finger,' said Granny in her gloomy voice, adding another row to her knitting, 'but you can't help thinking of Leaf Falling – must be desperate for a break from that oh-so-*tedious* research. Dipping into more exciting books must be *such* a temptation.' She shook her head and focused on her knitting, the needles flashing.

'Who knows what she might have taught herself. Those bunny ears were not kind.'

Seth was listening intently and was thinking of the bustling cafe, of the half-eaten cupcake and Myrtle Rust slumped against the window. Leaf Falling must be the name of the moss-haired girl.

Granny reached into her basket again and lifted out some almost-complete mittens in orange wool with green speckles. They were quite possibly the ugliest pair of mittens Seth had ever seen. She handed them to him.

'Er – thank you, I'll see Miss Young gets them.'

Granny Onabutter threw back her head with a chortle that started at her toes. 'She won't want 'em. But making little presents for everyone gives me an excuse to call in and see you all. I love having all you young people around, and poor Armory Opal, just a little out of his depth with all these pranks. I do what I can to help.'

'Armory Opal?' asked Seth.

Granny eyed Seth shrewdly. 'Our Apprentice Finder,' she explained, looking at Seth with undisguised curiosity. 'His job is to place people who have passed their Prospect with the right principal.' She put her head on one side. 'Surprised you haven't met him yet. Ah, but yes. You did say you haven't yet passed your Prospect. Very lucky to have landed yourself a month with Miss Young.'

She eased herself from the chair without waiting for a reply.

'You mark my words. Myrtle Rust has been struck down with sinister magic. Prank or no prank. I am going to make it my business to keep a watchful eye on all you lovely young people! We can only hope this isn't just the beginning of something really *ugly* happening in our lovely Gramichee.' She looked at Seth as she left. 'Let's hope Cheery's wrong, and that you haven't joined us at a really *nasty* time for the apprentices.'

PART TWO

7. Delicious Demise

Behind the counter there was a big blue clock with an unusual face. It followed the white crescents of the waxing and waning of the moon. It was far easier to see how far away they were from the next full moon than it was to actually tell the time.

For Seth, it felt like that clock had only one purpose – to count down the month and serve as a constant reminder of the precious little time he had in which to perfect a spell good enough to pass his Prospect.

'How long will Miss Young be away?' he asked Cheery, trying to put aside everything that Granny had just told them. 'What jobs should I be doing?'

'You will be thrilled that you can do all of 'em. Knock yourself out. Really is your lucky day. I've got a CWK lesson soon. I'll do my best not to knock you out when I practise on you when I get back. That was a joke, by the way,' said Cheery, picking up her well-thumbed novel. 'But you'll be pleased to know she'll be gone long enough for you to clear up. And tackle the tricky task of assembling ingredients for Sinful Skin.'

But before he could even start, a sound from outside had him and Cheery rushing to the window. They peered out curiously and were greeted by the strange sight of a cherubic golden-haired boy determinedly lobbing mud pies at the curorium next door. It looked as if an angel had escaped from a school nativity play to splatter the already dirty window with streaks of sticky mud and grit.

Cheery went straight outside and yelled. The miniature angel shook his golden curls and his fist at her and ran off.

'What was that all about?' Seth asked when she returned and stayed hovering by the window. 'Is this whole town angry and strange?'

'Herb Camphor,' Cheery sighed. 'Another apprentice. He's getting back at Calamus's apprentice for pranking him. Made his whole body go blue.' She covered her mouth to hide a secret smile. 'Quite a nice shade of blue. He did look funny.' But then she frowned. 'But Granny's right. These pranks . . .'

Seth was determined not to be sidetracked. 'Let's get on with Miss Young's ingredients – it was Fingernails Finest,' he corrected. 'Not Sinful Skin. I'll make a start.'

He was eager to explore the kitchen prep room, with its strange ingredients and racks of mixing bowls and weighing scales, and reminded himself how important it was to focus on this chance to learn magic.

He returned to the shop after uncovering two lists. The first was for Sinful Skin, so not what he needed. Seth studied the sprawling handwriting of the second, which didn't even have a title. 'Naja berries, glychwychyn, belladonna, acacia bark, alpaca calfsfoot jelly, trefoil root,' he managed to decipher. 'What do they all do? What magic are you learning?'

Cheery dragged herself away from watching the deserted Forum to give a half-hearted glance. 'You'll also need some of the unpleasantly sticky cream, which we keep in a vat in your *bedroom*.' Her light-brown eyes glinted. 'That stuff binds it all together, I think. The rest of it, haven't a clue. If it smells good, people seem determined to pay a fortune for it. I wanna learn magic, not how to rake in a ton of money by—' She bit her lip.

Then she waved at an untidy pile of papers kept vaguely in order by a brass paperweight shaped like a boxing rabbit. 'You're gonna need to dig out orders, see when it's all arriving. I might go for a lie-down. I have a double bed to spread out on. It's very comfy.' But she continued watching the square outside.

'Have you tried any? What does it all do, exactly? What about Miss Young's Perfectly Prime Powders?'

Cheery snorted. 'They've got a big label on saying to only take them once a day, yet she swigs it down like lemonade. Just goes to show.'

'Show what exactly?'

'You ask a lotta questions.'

'Well, I only have a month to learn something to get me past my Prospect.'

Cheery finally dragged herself away from the window and accompanied Seth to the kitchen prep room.

From the way she started slamming ingredients on to the worktop, he could tell Cheery was much more interested in the escalation of the pranks than she was in making Fingernails Finest.

'Leaf Falling put rabbit ears on Tendril Vetch? How serious is that?' Seth asked. 'Do you really think what happened to Myrtle was a prank?'

'You really do ask a lotta questions.' Cheery looked at Seth through narrow eyes. 'Well, Granny might be right about Leaf making the most of her time in the library to look up some super-wicked pranks. But let's just say I doubt she's mastered the magic to put Myrtle into a near-death coma, if that's what you're suggesting.'

'I wasn't suggesting anything.'

'Leaf is more likely to die of boredom than to learn any decent magic in her apprenticeship. She's in sorcerer chronology, poor fish. Her principal is Haddock Troutbean, father of the dismal Gloria. Now what happened to Gloria – that was seriously awful.'

Seth knew that name. And hearing it was so unexpected that the bowl he had been holding slipped from his grasp. Luckily it was made of plastic and simply bounced.

'What happened to Gloria?' he couldn't help but ask. 'Was she another victim of a magical prank?'

'No, what happened to Gloria was far worse,' said Cheery, roughly ladling out a dollop of sticky cream without bothering to weigh it.

Seth had first learnt of the whole world of magic when a bunch of sorcerers had arrived at the Last Chance Hotel. Gloria Troutbean had been among them. Her grandfather, Wintergreen, had been a famous sinister sorcerer. Seth didn't fancy Cheery finding out he knew any sinister sorcerers.

'The absolute worst,' went on Cheery. 'Gloria got turned down by every single principal in Gramichee. But then she does have about as much chance of doing magic as a mushroom. And as she's from one of the most ancient of the sorcerer families . . . cue total humiliation for the Troutbeans.'

Cheery prodded at the sprawling handwriting of the untitled list. 'All right. Where are we with this? "Calfsfoot jelly" sounds better than "boiled hooves", I suppose. People put it on their *faces*. Ugh! But, we've totally got none. You best toddle next door and ask them.'

'To the curorium?' asked Seth, remembering that darkened shopfront and the aroma of damp.

'S'right. They've a good chance of having spare ingredients. Seeing as Miss Young has stolen plenty of their business since she opened. But then would you go into an eerie shop that smells like a swamp and buy something from creepy Calamus who looks like he'd more likely poison you than cure you? Pretty much everyone has him fixed as being on the sinister side. Tendril had better be careful he's not going the same way. That shark Calamus went out just a tick ago. Hint: go now. Because anyone connected with Miss Young is not exactly popular with creepy Calamus.'

Seth barely had time to register that Tendril Vetch must be Calamus's apprentice. He took her advice and grabbed the list, thinking he had to impress Miss Young. He had to stop worrying about Tendril Vetch, Leaf Falling, Gloria Troutbean, or even poor Myrtle Rust. *Just focus on learning as much magic as you can – don't get drawn in to worrying about sinister pranks and this being a nasty time to be an apprentice.*

'Just watch out, Seth,' said Cheery in a warning voice, 'that Calamus doesn't turn you into a frog.'

Seth paused and Cheery fell into a peal of delighted laughter. 'Salmon and fishcakes! I'm joking! He only does frog-turning on the second Tuesday of every month.' She blinked at him, her eyes wide. 'If you're lucky, today he'll only turn you into a rabbit.'

8. CALAMUS THE CURIOUS CUROLOGIST

All thoughts of Myrtle Rust and any attacks on the apprentices were wiped from Seth's mind by the seeping, rotten bottom-of-a-pond smell he detected as he tried to open the badly sticking door of the curorium.

The windows were filmed-up like ancient eyes, making it impossible to tell if anyone was inside. He shoved the door again, harder, and was suddenly through, stumbling, blinking, aware of shelves clustering in on every side, looking up at dusty towers of dark jars and bottles.

In a way it was similar to the old-fashioned sweet shop secret entrance to Elysee headquarters. Except these crammed shelves offered far less promise of treats . . . earwig legs, woodlouse jelly . . . and a squat jar of what looked like little puffy alien maggots. Seth leant in a little closer. MARSHMALLOWS (WHITE), read the label.

As he breathed in an overpowering smell of pungent plants and firecrackers, it took a moment to notice a figure to one side, his back turned as he assembled bottles and herbs into a brown leather case, reading each label carefully and oblivious to Seth's entrance.

His well-worn black trousers and matching jacket seemed designed to make him blend in to the shop. The most striking thing about the old man was his bundle of white hair, which stuck out from his head at a multitude of angles.

Was this Calamus? Hadn't Cheery just said she'd seen him going out?

As Seth's heart dropped into his boots he caught on that she'd tricked him quite deliberately. Was it too late to back out now? He could picture her grinning in her beanbag, knowing he was going to have to ask a favour from the creepy curologist himself.

Seth could feel a rapid increase in his heart rate as he took a tentative step closer. Was he was about to speak to a sinister sorcerer? Could Calamus turn someone into a frog? Could anyone? Something was cooking up gently over a flame and Seth watched nervously as Calamus approached the bubbling saucepan. All Seth could detect was an odourless clear liquid.

The curologist reached inside a long cardboard box with skeletal fingers and took a smooth, round object in each hand before plopping them with precision into the bubbling mixture.

What were they? The eyes of an unfortunate creature? Seth felt sweat prickle on his brow. What sort of powerful concoction was being brewed? Was he watching a sinister magical spell in action? Just then, several wisps of smoke started pluming from behind a dark green curtain decorated with a golden dragon, drawn across a corner of the shop.

'Tendril!' Calamus called, without taking his eyes from the pan. 'You've not burnt it again?' He gave the first sign that he knew Seth was even there, turning so the dim light fell on the right side of his face, revealing skin puckered and an ugly raw pink, dimpled like orange peel. Near the jaw it was a livid red that looked terrifyingly as if it was melting.

Seth flinched away and was immediately embarrassed that he'd done so. Calamus must have been badly burnt in the past.

Tendril Vetch emerged through the curtain with two plates of heavily charcoaled toast. He was looking far less troubled than he had in the cafe.

'Do it again!' Calamus snapped at his apprentice, and then to Seth: 'You seem very fascinated by our supper.'

The sinister spell, Seth could see now, was two eggs in white shells delicately moving in boiling water. And the plume of smoke was definitely from burnt toast.

'What do you want?' barked the old man, just as Tendril, more politely, said: 'Can I help you?'

'You can help us all and open the back door to let some of that smoke out!' barked Calamus.

Seth explained, hesitantly, who he was and that Miss Young needed help with some hard-to-find ingredients.

Calamus responded with a nasty laugh. 'Miss Young thinks we are going to help? When she has set up business next door to me and gone about trying to tempt all my customers away? Interesting.'

Seth thought of the bright shop next door, Miss Young's breezy welcome, the smell of rosewater and gingerbread, the comfy seat where customers could sit and chat.

Tendril took Seth's list and peered at it. Seth wondered how he could read it in the dim light. He wondered how anyone could read anything and if customers ever ended up with the wrong potions.

'We've had difficulty getting some of these ingredients too,' the apprentice said, shaking his head and trying to return the list to Seth.

But Calamus reached out and snatched it with an ancient hand, bent and with yellowing fingernails like bird claws. 'Naja berries, glychwychyn, belladonna, acacia bark, alpaca calfsfoot jelly and trefoil root,' he read in his cracked voice. 'Not available, you say? Luckily, none of them are needed in our curlotions.'

His eyes narrowed and he looked at Seth accusingly. 'I hope no one's making a misguided attempt to fulfil the Oakmore Prophecy. There was me thinking her speciality was a dollop of fraud and a pinch of insincere magic.' The grey, hooded eyes of the elderly curologist were suddenly sharp. Instead of handing the crumpled paper back, he screwed it into a ball.

Seth knew he wasn't brave enough to insist on Calamus returning it. But something else was registering, and not just that Calamus didn't think much of Miss Young's magic. Seth was smart enough to work out that those ingredients must be things he shouldn't have asked for.

Cheery had conned him into thinking Calamus was out. And she must have made up a bogus list of doubtful ingredients for him to ask for. His face flamed.

'Er – thank you for your help, but I probably should be getting back.' He began to shuffle towards the door.

Seth was relieved to turn and slink back to the cloying but innocent smell of gingerbread and rose-water. He now had a new objective: start planning a way to get back at Cheery.

9. JUST TRY TO STOP ME

Neither Cheery's open hostility nor even what had happened to Myrtle Rust could stop Seth's joy that, at last, he was mixing with magical folk. It all had to help to improve his own magic. Surely.

Even a night in the hammock couldn't quite dent Seth's enthusiasm, although he found it impossible to drift off to sleep in his cramped lodgings. He lay awake, aware of the boiler thrumming away in the cellar beneath. He missed Nightshade, who was dutifully on mouse duty. Unable to bear the stuffiness any longer, he padded through to look through the dirty glass of the rear door, giving it a rub with his sleeve to look out. There might even be somewhere outside to hang his hammock.

The key was in the lock and in a moment he was through the door and surrounded by greenery so thick he could barely make out the high walls of the buildings surrounding the courtyard garden. Above, the sky was a friendly midnight, soft with stars that reminded him of the glow-worm glade in the Last Hope Forest.

He missed his home. But this was his big chance. He was going to make the most of it. And out here might be a safe place to practise his magic.

For a moment he focused on conjuring up a light, the way Angelique had tried to teach him. He concentrated on his hand and said the magical summoning word out loud: 'Sffera.'

He repeated the word. He said it louder and more strongly. Then he could see it, a tiny pinprick right in the palm of his hand. But the light flared into a flame, then swiftly became a jet of intense heat. He threw it away. Luckily it fell on a patch of damp earth. No harm done, but he groaned. Perhaps it was time to return to his hammock, even though his stomach grumbled and it would take ages to get comfortable enough to sleep.

Miss Young had been out all evening and her fridge contained only strange fruit, crispy leaves and a gloopy white substance that he was fairly sure was yogurt, but might just be an ingredient for one of her spells.

He hadn't wanted to ask Cheery about supper, not even when she popped out and returned with a delicious-smelling fat portion of freshly cooked chips that she proceeded to eat very slowly right in front of Seth, while he munched on a couple of biscuits found in a cupboard.

He tried to settle into the hammock again, and must have been more tired than he thought, because the next thing he knew Nightshade was prodding him needlessly hard with a claw, giving a huge pink yawn and muttering on about Calamus's cat, Useless Tom. It was morning, and Seth scampered to join Cheery for his first proper day at work.

But there was immediate disappointment when Miss Young grabbed her black bag and an array of white boxes. She disappeared off to do house calls in a flurry of urgent instructions, leaving a waft of rose-water and no update on when his magical training would start.

'How are we going to make anything if you failed

to get any of the ingredients from Calamus?' Cheery groaned convincingly about the bogus list, which Seth no longer even had. Cheery had given him a hard time about that. 'Not even naja berries? She's gonna be mad and I'll have to tell her it's your fault. They're wicked expensive, but Miss Young gets through stacks of them.'

For now Seth ignored the trick she'd played on him. He really had no choice other than to try to befriend her. 'What does she use them for? Is that why everything she sells costs so much?'

Cheery answered with another of her how-are-you-so-stupid looks.

He tried again. 'You don't seem all that interested in working here, and with your CWK you'd be really good at MagiCon – S3 maybe. Why did you get the apprenticeship here? What happened?'

'Well, who wouldn't want to be the girl who kicks the door in and rushes in to save the day? Of course I dreamt of being one of those cops you see on films who arrive at the bad guy's house, but Dagger Tour-maline happened.'

Cheery aimed a boot at a vat of sticky cream. It wobbled like a vast jelly, but at least it didn't crack and leave Seth with even more clearing up to do. 'Beat me to the MagiCon apprenticeship. He gets to work with one of the most powerful sorcerers ever and I got here. Dagger hasn't a clue half the time whether he's teaching him the right stuff or not. Inspector Pewter is wicked eccentric. But at least it's proper magic.'

It was all Seth could do not to show his surprise.

So the unkind boy at the cafe with eyes like jet was Inspector Pewter's apprentice.

And the inspector was one of the most powerful sorcerers ever?

Seth had been told before that his friend was an incredibly strong rudiment and could move air, water, even rocks with his bare hands. Seth had seen him do it. But he was also one of the kindest people Seth had ever met.

As Cheery went rattling on with another of the high-speed grumbles she specialized in, he found himself imagining an apprenticeship with Pewter. What a rollercoaster ride that would be. And he tried not to feel hurt that the inspector had never even hinted that an apprenticeship at MagiCon was possible. Of course, Dagger would have passed the Prospect, but hadn't Seth proved he was a reasonable detective?

'All I'm learning is how to sweep the floor and count her money!' Cheery suddenly blurted out. 'I was doing more magic sat in my bedroom getting my dolls to close their eyes. Every time I see Armory Opal I force myself not to let on what a load of hairy fishcakes this apprenticeship is. Should arrest myself for fraud.'

This hit Seth like a blow to the back of the head. 'You're not learning magic?'

Miss Young wasn't going to teach him? His chances of passing the Prospect had been slim before. Now, with Mrs Squerr and a deadline involved, his chances felt like they were crumbling like cake.

'She's too busy, or . . .' Cheery trailed off, and shot him a sideways guilty look.

But the chance to quiz Cheery further would have to wait, as a delightful tinkle from the door drew Seth to the front of the shop. He tried to put on a customer-friendly face and was surprised to find Tendril Vetch, his hood up, slinking in, giving an annoyed glance at the giveaway song from the charms and chimes.

'Brought you some of those things you asked for,' he said, not looking Seth in the eye, but placing three small packages wrapped in brown paper on the counter. 'We didn't have everything and some of it's kept in a locked cupboard, so we might have glychwychyn, but—'

'Thank you so much!' said Seth, seizing the packages, curious to see what it all looked like. 'This is so kind of you. I thought you didn't have any of it. You won't get into trouble, will you?'

Tendril shrugged. 'Probably. Calamus is mad as a snake that Miss Young opened up next door with her fancy expensive powders, and that she's taking away his customers even though she charges ten times as much.'

Seth busily unwrapped the parcels, sniffing a mass of dried berries, discovering a small container of white liquid and some fresh green herbs. He longed to know what they could all be used for. At least the cantankerous curologist would be teaching his apprentice some real magic.

'Your apprenticeship looks so interesting,' he said.

'Interesting?' Tendril laughed. 'Which bit? The horrible smell? The disgusting ingredients?'

'Isn't curology a sort of herbal healing?'

'That's exactly it!' Tendril smiled shyly. 'Everyone knows Calamus is the most talented curologist – even Dagger wanted an apprenticeship with him. I can put up with him being a bit creepy.'

'Is he creepy?'

'A bit. Quite a lot, actually.'

It didn't sound as if anyone had ended up with the apprenticeships they wanted. Seth felt sorry for Tendril, working cooped up with the irritable Calamus and the veil of suspicion that he dabbled in the sinister arts. Was that why Dagger and Leaf had been picking on Tendril in the Scrum?

But mainly he felt a deep envy. 'Sounds like you're the only apprentice being trusted to learn any real magic.' Seth re-wrapped the ingredients.

'I really am,' Tendril said in a whisper. 'Do you want to come over later and see?' He said it as if throwing in the invitation was sort of a joke, as if anticipating a rejection.

But Seth just beamed. 'I'll be there the minute we close. Just try and stop me!'

10. Leaving Me Failing

Seth, eager to go and watch Tendril's magic, kept an anxious eye on the blue phases of the moon clock.

Right at the end of the day, the delightful jingle of the doorbell announced a final customer, but his annoyance turned to delight when it was Angelique who came in.

'Is it all going well?' She was dressed in a dark suit with red lining that was not only smart, but fitted her so perfectly it enabled her to be deft and deadly effective when dealing with onslaughts from evil magic.

She couldn't stop her lip curling at the shelves of crystals and charms with their inflated magical claims and giving them a gentle prod with the end of her divinoscope.

'I've come to say goodbye. I've been called on a case.'

He should have guessed. Yet before he knew it, he'd said: 'You're going away?' He hadn't meant it to come out so shocked and disappointed, as if he was accusing her of leaving him to fail on his own. She'd neglected her work to help him and he reminded himself he had resolved he was going to do this without her.

'Angelique, you really don't need to worry about me. I won't fail. I'll make a success of this, just you see.' He smiled brightly. 'What's the case?'

'Very boring. Disappearance of a teacher.'

'I'm sure it'll be more interesting than watching me blow stuff up.'

She managed a small smile and unexpectedly slipped something into his hand. It felt like a rock worn by the sea, hard and smooth, but when he looked, it was a piece of glass, faintly frosted, with a surface glazed with crackles and a hole in the centre.

'If the moment comes, you'll be able to talk to me,' said Angelique.

'Erm, thanks, how exactly?' She had an impatient way of saying things, as if Seth would instantly understand. All Seth knew was that he was being handed something magical. He put it to his eye to look through the hole.

Angelique batted it away from his face. 'I said if the moment comes. It's a wave glass. I found them on the beach when we were at that lighthouse.' She held out her hand and he saw in her palm a stone so similar they might have been made together. 'I noticed them because they were nearly identical, almost like they came from the same bottle and managed to stay together. We'll get a really strong connection.'

'You mean I can use this like sending you a message in a bottle?'

'Something like that.' She smiled and twirled the red stripe in her hair with a finger. 'Well, best of luck, Seth.'

What could he say? 'Please don't give up on me.'

'Whatever makes you think I'd do that?'

But she didn't quite meet his eye. He knew how magical she was, how good at her job and how in demand. He knew what she did was both secretive and dangerous and a terrible feeling rose up that this was the last time he was ever going to see her. Cheery had planted plenty of doubts in his mind that he was going to learn much at all from Miss Young. And if he didn't pass his Prospect in a month's time, the magical world – and Angelique – might be closed to him for ever.

He wanted to speak, but was afraid of saying the wrong thing. He really should not stop her going. He put the wave glass in one of his many pockets and said something about being sure he wouldn't need it. Even as he said it, he knew a strong connection wouldn't be the problem. She'd be busy, she was always busy. And he'd be busy too. He had to perfect one bit of magic and time was running out.

'You will be fine, Seth.'

'Course I will. And if you need me for anything, you can call me too.'

She reached for the door and opened it, setting off the tinkling.

'I won't let you down, Angelique,' he said quickly.

'Course you won't.'

She stopped at the door, turned, and he wished he knew the right words to say a brave farewell that didn't give away how sad her going made him. He found a smile and waved the magical glass.

'In an emergency, Angelique, got it. I won't use it

for any prank calls, then.'

As final parting words, Seth wished he could have found something a lot better.

The door closed. He was going to have to realize his cherished dreams without Angelique.

11. Naja Berries and Swamp Buns

Seth made his way down the narrow passage that separated Calamus's business from the Belle Boutique and headed for the back door of the curorium.

As he arrived in the courtyard he was hit with a familiar smell of wild garlic that reminded him so much of home.

He felt excited but nervous. He was about to watch some magic being done. He squashed down what Cheery had hinted about Calamus, but it was worrying at his insides.

Creepy Calamus looks like he'd more likely poison you than cure you. Pretty much everyone has him fixed as being on the sinister side. Tendril had better be careful he's not going the same way.

But to Seth, Tendril had seemed friendly and generous – surely he wouldn't be involved in any sinister magic?

From above, the sounds of slinky, soulful jazz drifted down and Seth looked up to where a curtain billowed out of an open window at the top of a criss-crossing metal fire escape. The back door to the curorium was opened and Seth saw Tendril grinning an excited welcome.

'Granny Onabutter always practises her saxophone about this time,' Tendril said as he led Seth through the rear of the shop, which appeared to be full of ancient junk, past murky stairs and pushed through the dragon curtain.

The smell of bonfires and fireworks from his previous visit had receded and had been replaced by something strong and vegetably, slightly spicy. Like celery. Seth looked to see if there was a pan on the gas ring. Maybe they were making soup – a mound of herbs was half-chopped, a knife waiting next to them.

He took in everything. On the long wooden

workbench, worn smooth and pitted with years of use, was a pair of golden weighing scales and a neat arrangement of assorted phials and boxes. Seth was relieved that this time Calamus wasn't sitting there.

'Let's have tea first,' said Tendril, looking nervous.

Seth itched to take a closer look at one of the old and interesting books, one of which was open at a page of spidery writing that must be difficult to decipher, but he followed Tendril back into the garden, where they drank tea made with fresh leaves growing just by the back door. The evening air was filled with the pungent scent of herbs and the sound of the saxophone. Seth was soon examining a small, segregated leaf he didn't recognize.

'Is all of this used in your curology spells, Tendril?' Seth said, gesturing at the garden and thinking of all the things growing at home in the Last Hope Forest. All that magic that might be right there, growing tantalizingly close to his hotel.

Tendril smiled shyly and scratched his ear. 'My friends call me Ten for short. Most herbs you can use dried, but I'm finding the magic easier where I can use fresh. Just wish I was good at growing stuff. You know about plants, do you?' He bent to a plant that looked yellow and sickly, struggling to free itself from a rampant rosemary. 'Because this sugwort is essential in the medicine that stops me sneezing. It's not looking so good.' He showed Seth another patch where thick-stalked plants each had a cluster of small, very dark fruit. 'Or these. And these were going to make my fortune.'

'I've never seen anything like that before. What is it?' When Seth touched one of the berries, it felt hard as stone.

'If I'm lucky, soon they'll be naja berries. Quite rare.'

Seth put a finger in the soil where the thick stem of the plant met the earth and squinted up at the high brick wall that surrounded them, blocking the light.

'What are naja berries, exactly?' They'd been on that list of suspicious ingredients. 'I thought Calamus said they were the sort of ingredients he wouldn't use.'

Tendril explained he didn't plan to use them, but that they were valuable and in short supply. He thought he might sell them and make some money. 'But only if they grow well. How are you getting on with Cheery?' he asked.

Seth shrugged. 'Do any of the apprentices get on? I've heard you all play pranks on each other.'

'There might be a bit of rivalry,' replied Tendril evasively.

Seth prodded the dry, cold soil, trying not to

replay the scene in the Scrumdiddlyumptious Cafe: the crash of china, Glad's shocked face, hands clapped to her mouth. And Myrtle Rust being so deeply asleep Glad thought she was dead . . .

'Swamp buns!' a voice suddenly intruded from on high.

Seth looked up and saw the grey hair and bright eyes of Granny Onabutter peering at them over a wrought-iron balcony. Her skinny frame was dwarfed in an oversized scarf.

'I've been baking,' she trilled. 'I expect you lovely apprentices have just finished work and are hungry. Young people are always hungry!'

Tendril called up to her, 'Sorry, we have jobs to do, Granny. But thanks. She is very sweet,' he hissed to Seth, 'but – honestly – you'd think her swamp buns were made with stuff from Calamus's shelves, and the old leftover stuff at that.'

Seth had yet to find much food at the Belle Boutique and was tempted. 'Her cooking has to be better than her knitting.'

Tendril suppressed a giggle. 'I found a pair of awful gloves she'd knitted for me – she hid them in my pocket. They were kind of a rough, bobbly wool. I'm pretty sure her eyesight's not up to it. Last time I went for cakes it tasted like she couldn't work out which is the sugar and which is the bicarbonate of soda.'

'Shall we say five minutes?' called Granny. 'I had some biscuits too. Somewhere. Oops, think Gorgeous Tom has gone and sat on them.'

'Tom is Calamus's cat,' said Tendril. 'Big ginger fluffball. Seems to prefer being up there with Granny or next door with Miss Young to being down here in the curorium.' A mouse scampered quite unafraid across Tendril's foot. 'Think he's afraid of the mice. There are quite a few.'

'Nightshade calls him Useless Tom,' Seth said without thinking.

'Nightshade?'

'Er –' Seth needed to change the subject, fast. He distracted Tendril by pointing at Granny's apartment. The balcony was bathed in a warm, evening light. 'Might be worth the risk of a swamp bun or two if you can persuade her to put a few of your naja berries up there,' he suggested. 'If you grab me a trowel, we could transplant them – they need more light.'

'All right, thanks. A swamp bun for my naja berries,' groaned Tendril. 'On our way, Granny Onabutter,' he called up, then whispered to Seth, 'But definitely don't eat the biscuits.'

12. A MAGIC HE LONGED FOR

A couple of swamp buns later, they were back in the curorium. 'So, I've got this curlotion to prepare for my sneezing – wanna help?' said Tendril, burping softly after digesting one of Granny Onabutter's soggy and green-tinged buns.

'Calamus lets you do it by yourself?' Seth couldn't keep the excitement and envy out of his voice. 'Your magic must be pretty good.'

'I wish! I often have to pour it away and start over.'

'Well, I blow things up.' He thought of the

93

puckered skin of Calamus's face. 'Is that how Calamus got his scars? Doing magic?'

'You actually think I've dared to ask him?' Tendril grinned.

Seth tried not to look too eager as they headed to the workbench and Ten opened a heavy book with gold edges and lots of complicated pictures. He ran a finger down a list of ingredients and stared up at the shelves with a frown as he began to bring down various bottles and jars.

Seth's keen nose inched closer as he watched Tendril's every move. It was a really complicated spell that involved not only many unusual ingredients but specified the exact material the knives and cooking vessels should be made of.

'It's like the most complicated recipe ever,' said Seth. Tendril must possess a magic that Seth longed for. He didn't let on that so far the most dangerous part of his own job was working the finger-snapping till. 'Did you start your apprenticeship at the same time as the others?'

'A bit before. Calamus hasn't taken an apprentice for ages.' Tendril rejected a bowl made of walnut and substituted one of glass. 'Maybe it's like cooking – Calamus says it's only a matter of following instructions. But then I burn toast. He always watches me.

Luckily, this spell is only for me.'

Seth didn't want to distract Tendril, but everything about the curorium fascinated him. Seth pointed to a bent leather bottle on an otherwise empty shelf. Attached was a label that said simply: FISH. 'What's that?'

'That shelf's for the finished spells for collection, and that one is for someone who always likes to take a little magic along with him when he goes fishing,' said Tendril, frowning over a dandelion root. 'Calamus does a few charms as well. He's very talented.'

'I think when it says to dice that dandelion root, it means cubes rather than slices,' put in Seth, reading the spell through and watching every move.

'Ah, thanks. Calamus has been experimenting with curlotions for my sneezing. Took him ages to get it right and it uses a few hard-to-find ingredients, and then I went and lost the jade bottle I carry it in.'

Seth recalled in the cafe how difficult Tendril had found it to stop sneezing once he started.

'Thought I'd redo this myself while he's out on his rounds. He's visiting these sick twins over at St Joanne's Walk. But it's complicated.'

'It says stir six times clockwise and six anticlockwise,' pointed out Seth as Ten picked up a beechwood spoon.

Tendril turned. 'Hey – I think you're better than me at this. It says to use a *tsp* of dried marigold seed, but I haven't a clue how much that is.'

Seth measured a careful teaspoonful, then Tendril invited him to take his place at the mixing bowl while he laboriously cut the dark green figweed into heavy chunks.

'It says finely chopped – I think we can get it a little finer than that,' said Seth, taking the copper knife from Tendril. He quickly shredded the fresh leaves and sprinkled them in the circular motion the spell asked for.

Together they poured over the crusty page and gradually the spell was put together. Seth checked the timing exactly as they left it to simmer, but he was feeling hot and a little faint.

'I think you might need to leave it another thirty seconds.' Seth stopped Tendril's hand as he went to remove the potion from the heat. He wiped his brow.

'Thanks again. Do you know, that looks exactly—' Tendril's face broke into a smile, which fell immediately. 'Seth . . . Seth, can you hear me?'

Tendril's words seemed to be coming through a fog. Seth was barely aware of the apprentice waving a hand in front of his face. The room came gradually into focus, as if he was coming out of a trance, or back from a long journey. How long had he been here for? He didn't even remember reaching the end of the spell. The air seemed too heavy to breathe and he was sweating, longing to be in the cool of the courtyard.

He tried to stagger to his feet. Tendril was waving a bottle in front of him. 'You all right? I think, together, we just did brilliant magic.' His eyes gleamed with triumphant fire.

13. AN ATTACK ON LEAF FALLING

Seth wasn't the only one feeling tired the next morning.

Miss Young's breakfast had been to guzzle more of her powders. She asked Cheery to open up the shop, saying, 'I don't like leaving you alone so much. One must make sacrifices for one's patients, of course, and the twins need as much care as I can give them. But these house calls are *exhausting*.'

Seth had actually been pleased Miss Young had been out visiting patients when he'd returned yesterday evening. Cheery had been in her room, so he'd been able to slip off to his uncomfortable hammock and had sunk almost immediately into a deep sleep.

He'd felt so sick and woozy in the curorium. Seth thought he remembered Tendril saying Calamus had told him he was also out making house calls. So much of the previous evening was now a fog.

But no sooner had Cheery turned the sign to 'open' than the bell tinkled and Seth had no time to feel exhausted or to remember the previous evening more clearly. Granny Onabutter's wrinkled little face beamed as she sprang in, bringing a burst of cool spring air, along with obvious excitement.

She approached the counter, curranty eyes alight. Seth, Cheery and Miss Young took a step back. 'There was another one last night!' she breathed.

'Another . . . ?' Miss Young frowned in confusion.

'She means another attack on an apprentice,' said Cheery.

Granny nodded and jabbed at Gorgeous Tom, who unfurled himself from the red lips chair with an angry hiss.

She settled into the chair, reached into her wicker basket for some half-finished multicoloured gloves and, once she'd started rattling her needles in enjoyment, said: 'I'll tell you everything I know.'

Which turned out to be not very much.

The attack had been on the chronicler apprentice, Leaf Falling, who worked in an office in the bustling Elysee headquarters under Haddock Troutbean. The girl with the moss-green hair, Seth remembered, who had given Tendril the rabbit ears.

'Discovered hit with a curse there's no shifting. Fast asleep when she was supposed to have gone home at the end of the day. Another carted off to Ward 23 with a Deathly Slumber. Just like Myrtle Rust!' said Granny. 'This is no accident and I'm not going to be the only one saying I'll be thinking twice about an apprenticeship for my granddaughter in Gramichee now.'

'Did no one see anything?' said Miss Young.

The mention of the magical hospital ward where his mother was a patient felt like a little stab in Seth's heart. He had been told it was best not to visit, but no one seemed inclined to tell him exactly why. This only meant his imagination went completely wild.

Cheery turned to him. 'Hey, looks like there might now be vacancies with Quartz Darkheart and Haddock Troutbean. And of all the apprenticeships in all of Gramichee, you had to walk in on mine.'

Miss Young wrung her hands. 'It's all an accident. These apprentices don't really yet know the power of magic.'

Granny Onabutter paused in her knitting to lean closer. 'Who's teaching the sinister magic around here? None of them should even know how to do a spell like that!'

Granny all but squealed as two dark shapes strode past the window. 'Ooh, MagiCon are going next door!'

She leapt out of the lips chair and dashed through the door, stuffing her multicoloured knitting into her wicker basket as she went.

'And the first place they call is the curorium,' said Cheery, heading straight to the window, with Miss Young and Seth following and unashamedly craning their necks.

Miss Young pushed the door ajar in case there was a chance to hear anything. 'Is it Calamus they're talking to?' she frowned. 'There have been rumours. But surely—'

'Or is it Tendril Vetch?' suggested Cheery. 'Leaf played a prank on Vetch. D'you think Dagger Tourmaline suspects he scoured old Calamus's spellbooks to pick up some sinister trick to get his revenge?' She used the bottom shelf of crystals to lever herself up to get a better view, and flattened her cheek against the glass.

Dagger rapped on the door to the curorium, but got no answer. They all watched as he smoothed back his dark hair, swished his black cloak around himself and pushed hard on the door.

'Someone should tell him that he should drop that cloak and get some sun, otherwise he might end up with a stake through the heart,' said Cheery, her eyes glued to what was happening next door.

'He looks rather handsome,' twittered Miss Young.

But Seth was watching the man next to him. Dagger looked short next to Inspector Pewter, who kept his head down and his hands deep in his pockets.

Dagger took a boot to the door, but not without a furtive glance that told Seth he was aware he had an audience. Three hefty kicks failed to budge it. His pale face was disappointed, but his jet-black eyes determined, and he positioned himself to put a shoulder in next.

Then it opened, revealing Calamus, his puckered face livid. 'Please, just a little patience for an old man.'

Dagger narrowly avoided falling through the doorway and was forced to steady himself. He straightened his swooshy cloak and cleared his throat. 'We need to question you about your movements yesterday evening.'

'So it *is* Calamus they want to talk to,' said Cheery as Dagger and Pewter followed the curologist inside.

'Shame we won't hear anything,' said Miss Young, pressing her delicate nose to the glass. She looked down at her hands and went to grab a tube of Delicious Demise she kept tucked in next to the till.

Nightshade slipped in. Seth thought she'd be catching up on her snooze time after a night chasing mice and picked her up and tickled her behind her ears, putting his ear close to her face.

'You might not be able to slip next door and listen in,' she purred in a very low voice right in his ear. 'But I can.'

She slinked back out and slipped in next door just before it was firmly closed.

Now all he could do was rely on Nightshade to find out what was going on.

14. KILLS OR CURES

The door remained closed for so long they gave up watching. The next time the tinkling of the bell drew them to the front of the shop a short gentleman was prodding a fat finger through the display of protective amulets and lucky charms.

'Mr Opal!' greeted Cheery.

The man turned and Seth recognized the stripy suit, tight-fitting waistcoat and bat-wing hair – it was the man he'd sat alongside in the Scrum. And he remembered the name. Armory Opal. Granny had called him the Apprentice Finder, the man who matched principals to the apprentices. The one who was out of his depth, unable to stop all the pranks.

'Hello, hello, young Cheery. And hello, other young man.' Opal's bat-wing hair drooped and the buttons on his gold-striped waistcoat were done up wrongly.

'Any news on Leaf?' asked Cheery. 'Was she hit with the same curse as Myrtle Rust? Is it the same person behind both spell attacks, d'you think?'

Mr Opal gave a heartfelt sigh. 'I have to trust MagiCon know what they are doing. They don't tell you anything. Calls have started from hysterical parents demanding to know if their children are safe. I had to get out of my office.'

'Perhaps you should give all your apprentices one of those?' Cheery suggested, nodding to the small amber bottle Mr Opal was fidgeting with.

He peered at the label, as if noticing he was holding the bottle for the first time. '*Protect your loved ones and survive*? Survive? Let's hope it doesn't come to that.' He approached the counter, looking up at the towering white boxes, and requested some Perfectly Prime Powders. 'My dear better half says she has soft hands like a baby from using your Delicious Demise and has heard good things about these too.' His eyebrows raised at the price of the slim packet handed to him. 'It's very small for that amount, isn't it?' he said, digging deep in a pocket and producing a fistful of notes, which he counted slowly.

'What you think, Mr Opal?' said Cheery. 'You know everything about the apprentices. You think an apprentice could have pulled off the magic?'

Seth had to admit that Cheery was good at this, leaning forward, opening her eyes with an innocent curiosity that disguised just how cleverly she was probing.

How had the curse been done? Surely someone would have needed to get close. And the attacks had happened at the cafe and at the Elysee ... that meant it had to be someone who would be familiar with those places. But that was probably most people in the magical world.

Armory considered. 'Turning Herb Camphor blue was a terrible prank. I only managed not to have to report that as illegal use of magic because it lasted less than six minutes.' He shook his head, making his bat-wing hair attempt a final launch, and wiped a sheen from his face. 'Whoever has cursed those poor girls must own up. The sooner we find out what magic they have been struck with, the sooner the medics on Ward 23 can cure them.' He fixed Cheery with a fierce look.

'You think I might know who it was?' Cheery was taken aback. 'So, you do think it *is* an apprentice?'

Mr Opal darted a nervous glance towards the curorium, passing a hand over his sweaty face. 'Whoever is responsible needn't be dealt with harshly. It was probably just a prank. But these pranks! They have got out of hand.' He darted a further nervous glance next door. 'They must stop! And they'll blame me if Calamus has been teaching Tendril something he shouldn't. The apprentice scheme has been so successful. Particularly for those from non-magical backgrounds. It must continue. Someone must own up!'

The second he left, Cheery turned to Seth: 'Well, that's just code for him blaming Tendril. And he thinks I know what Ten has been up to.'

'Do you think it's Ten?'

'I think it's looking bad. And all that *the apprentice scheme has been terrific for people from a non-magical background*. Yeah, Myrtle's thrilled. Passed the Prospect. Now asleep in Ward 23 with no sign of ever waking – welcome to the magical world!'

'She's from a non-magical family?' Seth asked. He wasn't sure why he was quite so surprised. He was also wondering how Ten was faring – no doubt he was being questioned at that moment.

Miss Young had found the tension too much, had declared a headache and was resting upstairs. She'd left instructions to assemble ingredients for more Delicious Demise. But neither Seth nor Cheery felt much like doing any work.

Seth was about to make a start when he was interrupted by the sounds of Pewter and Dagger Tourmaline leaving the curorium. He darted to the window.

Ten had been so kind. How could Seth not feel involved despite all his determination to steer well clear of any trouble and focus only on passing his Prospect?

'We don't make people ill,' snarled Calamus from the doorway. 'You won't find evidence we dabble in cursed potions or sinister magic of any kind here. Because it's obvious all we offer is *cur*lotions. Cures!'

'There is nothing more deceptive than an obvious fact,' responded Pewter mildly.

Dagger flapped his cloak about in a grand manner, until Cheery caught his eye and beckoned him into the Belle Boutique with an offer of tea. He swooshed past Seth and disappeared with Cheery into the kitchen prep area. Seth hovered. He was torn between trying to find out what Dagger might tell Cheery and trying to listen to Pewter and Calamus.

'Unless your plan is just to stick this on us, Sagacious – I know your ways too well.' Calamus jutted his scarred features into the inspector's face.

Seth had never heard anyone use Inspector Pewter's first name before. The two must know each other well, and it didn't exactly appear they were friends.

'No advantage to me sticking it on anyone unless these pranks stop,' said Pewter, not sounding the least bit annoyed by the insinuation. 'If it will make you happier, I can leave the apprentice investigation to Dagger. I'm sure he'll be glad of the chance to prove himself.'

Calamus answered with a sneering laugh. 'Yes, duck out of any responsibility, you'd like that. So sorry, but you'll have to work harder to pin it on us. I can give my young assistant an alibi. I was with him all yesterday evening. Go bother someone else.'

But Seth knew what Calamus had just told the inspector was a lie. Seth had gone next door to the curorium straight from work. And Calamus had not been there. Hadn't Granny said Leaf had fallen into a Deathly Slumber at the end of the day?

That lie exposed Calamus as a better suspect for the attack than Tendril.

Seth wanted to tell the inspector, but as he tried to get a clear picture in his head of exactly what had happened the previous evening, the more the memory slid away from him. His brain had felt foggy and he'd come over faint and sick and he couldn't be sure of anything, certainly not how long he'd stayed.

'You are saying we are barking up the wrong tree, looking at the apprentices?' Seth heard Pewter ask.

'It's your investigation, why should I even have an opinion?'

'Because I would thank you for it, Calamus.'

'What you are dealing with is ingestible potions bewitched by sinister curses,' grumbled the old man. 'I doubt even the Sorcerer General, Count Boldo Marred himself, would find that easy.'

He slammed the door.

Seth's ears pricked up again. This was another name he recognized. Count Marred had been another of the guests at the Last Chance Hotel when Seth had first learnt of the whole world of sorcery. It was news to him that the count was now Sorcerer General of the Elysee. That meant he had taken over as head of the magical world.

The inspector strode off with his great long legs, and any chance for Seth to tell him he knew Calamus had been lying was gone.

Seth heard the low voices of Cheery and Dagger. He hesitated. He'd promised himself to stay out of trouble and to concentrate only on his magic, but that was before his new friend had got into hot water. He might find out more if he could hear what Cheery and Dagger were saying.

15. Secret Information

By the time Seth had crept close enough to hear the conversation in the kitchen, Cheery was already rattling on, offering tea and biscuits and even a discount on Miss Young's most expensive products. Seth admired how expertly she was lulling Dagger into trusting her with as much insider Magi-Con information as she could squeeze out of him.

'I know where Leaf worked,' she was saying. 'It was on the edge of a busy corridor, people passing all the time. You must be having a right nightmare narrowing down leads.'

'I'm not going to reveal classified information, Cheery.'

'Course not! I wouldn't dream of asking you. With two apprentices now in Ward 23 . . . if there's anything I can do to help, let me know. Guess you don't have a clue yet on the spell? Or a main suspect? Shame for you. Your first big case.'

Seth was impressed how coolly she was playing it. He really hoped the pair wouldn't realize they were being overheard, and hoped just as much that no customer arrived right now to stop him listening in. He dared to peer round the kitchen door.

Dagger slammed his hand on the worktop. 'But I'm *this* close to solving it. I will be known as the one who cracked the Apprentice Assassin.'

'Apprentice Assassin!' said Cheery with a throaty chuckle. 'Turn it down a notch, Dagger. No one's died. But MagiCon must be freaking. Do they think it's the same person striking down the apprentices? Do they think someone is going after them one by one?'

Dagger leant in, took two more biscuits and dropped his voice. 'Can I trust you? I might need some help, because we know exactly who is behind these attacks.'

She picked up her mug and clinked Dagger's teacup in a toast. 'Well, MagiCon had better be ready for someone as awesome as you! Course you can trust me. Who is it?'

There was a long pause before Dagger went on: 'It's someone who's learning from a powerful sorcerer with a very sinister past. I have to stop him. But I can't make an arrest. I need to break his alibi!'

'Tendril?' Cheery failed to cover her surprise. 'That's some serious curse. Tendril Vetch could never've managed it.'

'No – we *know* he did it!' Dagger insisted with a confidence that chilled Seth.

Calamus had accused the MagiCon detectives of trying to put the blame on him and his apprentice, and it sounded as if that was exactly what Dagger intended. But the more Seth tried to remember exactly what time he'd headed to the curorium, what time he'd left, the more he got that feeling like a fog had settled on his brain. What had really gone on yesterday evening? He couldn't be completely sure of anything.

'Herb Camphor being turned blue – I'm sure that was Vetch,' Dagger went on. 'That's why Leaf put those furry ears on him, which made us all laugh at him. Vetch has been thirsting for revenge.'

'Yeah, we laughed at his bunny ears. You laughed harder than most. But longing to get your own back doesn't mean turning into the Apprentice Assassin.'

Dagger snatched Cheery's wrist and held it in a painful-looking grasp, pulling her towards him. 'Who got the apprenticeship with MagiCon? You'd do well to remember.'

'Sure, Dagger. But I can't be helpful, can I, if you don't tell me everything,' Cheery replied coolly. 'You got something good on Tendril?'

Seth was familiar enough with Cheery's martial arts skills to know that she could easily have batted off Dagger's aggressive move. But she submitted weakly, let him draw her right up close to his handsome pale face. He spoke in a quiet, cold voice.

'We have evidence. Clear evidence that places Vetch at the scene of the crime. Then that old man ruined everything by giving him an alibi. All I have to do is break that old man's lies. It would be really useful, Cheery,' he didn't relax his grip, 'if you had seen Vetch going out.' Finally Dagger released her and waited.

'I might be able to remember I saw that,' Cheery said. After a pause, she remembered to smile sweetly, but the fact that it was more of a grimace told Seth how much that smile cost her. 'But part of being a good magicop is having something to trade. Way I'm thinking, if this evidence was any good you'd have arrested him right away. You tell me – what exactly have you got on Vetch?'

Seth heard the young detective's hesitation.

'All right. But this goes no further.'

He dropped his voice to a whisper and Seth risked moving a step closer.

'We found something at the scene – something that was dropped by whoever cursed Leaf. That little jade bottle Tendril never goes anywhere without – we found that right beside her sleeping body.'

16. Leave it To The Experts

Seth knew instantly that Dagger was talking about the bottle that contained Tendril's curlotion. But Ten had said he'd lost it. That was why Seth had helped him to make more.

Had someone pinched the bottle and planted it to make him look guilty? Was someone setting out to pin these attacks on Tendril?

Right away, Seth knew what he had to do. And it was far easier to do it while Cheery was busy, rather than run the risk of having to explain. Glancing at the blue moon clock, he wondered how quick he could be.

He scribbled a note and left it by the till. *Had to go out.*

He headed for the door, then dashed back and added the word *sorry*, before almost tripping over a dark shape as he turned to leave again.

'Oi, there's me risking being trodden on by everyone and suddenly you've got better places to be? Thought you'd be keen to hear everything I've got to tell you,' growled Nightshade.

'Have to get to the Scrum. Come on.'

Nightshade grumbled that all she really wanted was a lie-down somewhere warm, but she trotted on her four paws alongside him and quickly understood the rush when he explained why he was keen to head to the cafe.

'You think someone pocketed it deliberately that time you were there in the cafe, thinking it would be great to point the finger?' said Nightshade. 'Then you need to remember who was there at the time. They're your suspects.'

'Tendril definitely had it in the Scrum. He was sneezing.' Seth was picturing the scene. 'Leaf was there. Don't expect she cursed herself. Dagger—'

'He seems a nasty piece, and very full of himself.

Love it to have been him. If you'd let me out of that basket I could have been so useful. As it was, couldn't see a dratted thing. Glad Tidings definitely had hold of the bottle? She could easily have swiped it.'

They skirted the wide central square of Gramichee, heading for the bright umbrellas that marked out the cafe.

'Gladys? Yes, I suppose so. And the Apprentice Finder, Mr Opal, was there. He's more likely than an apprentice to have conjured that Deathly Slumber spell. It's really sophisticated magic.'

'Whiskers and white mice, Seth, use your noodle. Why would the Apprentice Finder go about wiping out his own apprentices?'

'Yeah, but what motive could anyone have?'

But even Seth's limited understanding of the world of sorcerers told him how controversial the apprentice scheme was. It sadly wasn't difficult to imagine someone wanting to target the apprentices.

'Lots of people reckon that opening up apprenticeships to anyone who could demonstrate they have a spark of magic is the only way to save magic,' he said. 'But it's not been popular with everyone.'

'Course not – especially among some of the oldest sorcerer families. Too many of them have difficulty proving they still have that spark of magic,' said

Nightshade. 'And they hate the fact that others from outside can prove they are more magical.'

Seth could smell the welcoming cinnamon and sugar of the cafe in the air as they neared. But today he was thinking less about food and was busy trying to make sense of everything. As they passed Dark-heart's, Seth could not quite resist pausing to glance at the magical objects in the window. A tiny, golden bejewelled Scarab beetle, likely from Egypt, caught his eye – *to ward off evil spirits*, claimed the label. It didn't look any more genuinely magical than Miss Young's Worry Wiggles.

'This is where Myrtle Rust is an apprentice,' he whispered. 'She's not from a magical family. The apprentice scheme is causing all kinds of arguments. Do you think that could even be the reason apprentices are being attacked? I found out that Count Marred is now—'

'Sorcerer General – bossing it in the magical world,' said Nightshade. 'Funny, but no one was that keen to take over after the last chief was murdered. You're right – these apprentices are at the centre of a lot of trouble that goes right to the heart of the magical world.'

'How do you know these things, Nightshade?'

'I keep my whiskers close to the ground to help

you. But you could also help me, you know. You wanna use your detective skills – get to the bottom of there being so many mice. Miss Young's little furry problem is not natural. It's wearing me out.'

Seth found himself staring with curiosity at a strange glass item, halfway between a paperweight and a compass. TO IDENTIFY THE PRESENCE OF GHOSTS, SPIRITS AND GHOULS. There was also a chunky pointed stone, smaller than a closed fist, flaunting an outrageously hefty price tag and the dubious claim to be the carved tooth of a dragon.

'Getting your magic sorted is all you should be worrying about,' said Nightshade.

'Well, you help clear up how Tendril's bottle was found at the scene and I'll—'

'Can I remind you, Seth, going into the Scrum, asking questions – it's not what you're supposed to be doing.'

If Nightshade hadn't sounded so cross, Seth might have shared how he thought he might finally have done magic the previous evening.

But had he? Once before, he thought he might have done magic. That had been on a windswept clifftop when things had been going badly, and he thought he'd lost something to the bottom of the sea. Even then he hadn't been sure.

Last night he hadn't caused an explosion. If Ten was right, was there a chance he might finally be close to passing his Prospect?

But what if Tendril was hauled away for attacking people with sinister magic?

'I don't like this place,' Nightshade went on. 'I don't think we should hang around waiting for you to get attacked.'

Seth shrugged off her comment and pressed on through the sunny umbrellas, pausing outside the cafe door. 'So what did you learn by keeping your whiskers to the ground and sneaking into the curorium?'

Nightshade gave an enormous pink yawn and stretched her claws. 'Your inspector asked a load of questions about what curse might have been used. Calamus got tetchy. Told Pewter he should know better and that he shouldn't be harassing him every time he wants all the inside info on how sinister magic was cast. How was he supposed to run a legit business? he said. They don't get along, those two.'

Seth made up his mind. 'Nightshade, I-I think I did magic, with Tendril, last night,' he said quickly.

'Well, hope you don't mind if I don't come in for a celebratory ice cream. Why d'you have to pick someone apprenticed to a sorcerer with a very iffy reputation to teach you magic? Hope you're not getting drawn into any sort of dark power, Seth.'

'I am not drawn to dark power!'

Was he drawn to Tendril Vetch because he possessed a dark power?

It was only when Nightshade said: 'You heard from her?' that Seth looked into his hand and realized he was playing with the wave glass Angelique had given him. 'Know how to use that thing?' she added.

'Nope.'

'Well, how difficult can it be? Give it a try. She'd want to know all this.'

'I'm waiting for her to call me.'

'Yeah? Is that because you know what she'd say if she was here now? She'd say if you're only going to learn magic from some boy with a dark power, leave right now. If apprentices are being attacked – leave right now. Anyway, you may as well get inside, as you won't listen to me. But one thing we do know is that this place is not too friendly to cats. Think of that as you tuck into a pile of doughnuts.' She stalked off, tail in the air.

17. TRICKERCHOCKERGLORY

Two days ago, Glad Tidings had been mostly one big smile. Today her welcoming grin was more the desperate grimace of someone who had spent her day staring at empty tables and a pile of freshly made cinnamon buns growing cold and stale.

A whole fine array of decorated cakes lay untasted. There was no comforting gurgle of coffee bubbling and milk being frothed. And no one was sitting around doing the crossword while munching on a crusty baguette.

Seth didn't know what to say. News must have spread quickly about Myrtle Rust being mysteriously struck down with a sinister curse while eating here.

The only customer Glad had to smile at was Seth. He was ready with one in return and didn't even need to pick up a menu. 'I'd like to try one of those frothy green drinks, please.'

He admired Glad's determination to keep on going and had to steel himself to put to her the questions he'd come here to ask. It was true that Glad herself would have had plenty of chance to palm that bottle. And he'd had plenty of warnings from both Angelique and Pewter: treat everyone as a suspect.

'A friend of mine lost something,' he began quickly, before he lost his nerve. 'A small jade bottle? Have you seen it?' He watched her face for any signs: a flicker either of guilt or uncertainty.

He was aware of the door opening with a rush of fresh air. Finally, another customer. But Seth kept his eyes fixed firmly on Glad.

Her smile only broadened. 'You're a friend of Tendril Vetch? That's great! He *is* the one who's lost that bottle?'

Seth nodded.

'Well, if I'd seen it I'd have been outta that door to hand it right to him. I know how much he needs that medicine. You gonna order anything to eat with that, honey?'

Before he could reply, Seth felt a solid hand on his shoulder: 'Young Seth here is no mean chef himself. If you ever get a chance to try his shortbread – take it. Today, I am going to buy Seth one of your specials please, Glad.'

'Inspector Pewter!' Seth avoided meeting his eyes, because sometimes when Pewter looked at you directly it became hard to look away, however much you wanted to.

Glad closed her notepad, stuck her pencil behind her ear and bustled off. 'A very good choice, if I do say so.'

'An astonishingly able chef,' muttered Pewter, taking a chair and steepling his fingers on the table in front of him. 'And with the potential to be a reasonable sorcerer. As long as he doesn't get distracted. Either you asking about a jade bottle is a remarkable coincidence, or you have infiltrated what is supposed to be part of a highly secret, top-level MagiCon investigation.'

'I thought it was just pranks.'

'You weren't supposed to think anything.'

'I was just asking about that jade bottle for a friend,' Seth said lamely, taking a seat opposite Pewter.

Glad appeared with a tall dish crammed with layers of strawberry and mango, ice cream and double-choc sauce, topped with fairy sprinkles, along with a glass full of fresh green frosty-looking froth. Seth's stomach responded with a rumble of delight.

'Say hello to the trickerchockerglory,' she trilled as she placed both in front of him. 'Word of warning. Don't be surprised when you get to the bottom – the last spoonful warms your lips. You'll like it after eating all that ice cream.' She bent low, so when she said the words they came out as warm breath on his ear. 'It's magic.'

She placed a pot of tea shaped like a penguin in front of Pewter, and headed back to the counter.

'I might have overheard Dagger and Cheery talking,' said Seth, deciding how best to eat his fabulous dessert. 'This looks incredible. Miss Young's fridge is mostly frilly lettuce.'

'And I suppose you couldn't prevent your infernal cat hanging around the curorium?' said Pewter. He really didn't miss much. 'How is it going?'

Seth wasn't quite sure if Pewter was asking about his one-month trial for an apprenticeship with Forever Young, or his chances of passing the Prospect. Or his magic. Sadly the answer to all of these was the same: badly.

He nibbled a small spoonful of chocolate-smothered ice cream first. He wanted to make the sundae last as long as possible, and to dodge the inspector's question as long as possible too.

'You mean my thoughts about your case?' Seth suggested hopefully.

Pewter leant forward. 'I meant I'd appreciate your thoughts on the finest ice cream and chocolate laced with the finest magic. Your glorious tricker-chockerglory.'

'Oh. Yes, it's delicious.'

'You don't seem as completely wowed by magical ice cream as I anticipated. The day you stop taking a deep interest in food, Seth, is the day I know things are not good. Hmm, so you're taking an interest in my case. Why does that not surprise me? The question is . . .' Pewter's spoon clinked as he stared into the distance, stirring his tea, suddenly lost in his own thoughts.

Seth hardly expected the inspector to talk freely, even though he desperately wanted Pewter to trust him with a few details of the case. He focused on sampling the green frothy drink next. It tasted a little of chocolate, a little of strawberry, of orange, bitter and sweet all at the same time. And he became very intent on savouring a mouthful of cold ice cream with warm chocolate sauce, trying to identify all the ingredients.

The inspector gave himself a little shake. 'You have a grand gift for silence, Seth. It makes you quite invaluable as a companion. As well as your gift with shortbread. This is definitely a three-shortbread problem.'

'These pranks?'

'Pranks, as you say, Seth.'

'Leaf gave Tendril Vetch long furry ears like a rabbit. Armory Opal said someone turned Herb Camphor blue, and that that was almost banned magic.' Seth omitted Cheery and Dagger's insistence that Ten had been behind that prank. 'How good at magic would you have to be to do those things? And what about the Deathly Slumber curse? Could that just be a prank gone wrong?'

Pewter sipped his tea. 'It is my business to know what other people do not know. But why am I getting the impression you know a little too much? Rabbit ears and turning people the wrong colour is not such advanced magic as you might think.'

Seth's immediate thought was how incredibly pleased he'd be if he could magic a pair of rabbit ears on anyone, or turn them blue. But it was not good to wish yourself using magic for unkindness and tricks. He couldn't stop a small sigh escaping, and not just because he was reaching the end of his tricker-chockerglory and felt the promised warm blush of magic on his cold lips.

Everyone else seemed so effortlessly good at magic.

If he wanted the inspector to share anything, he should offer up some information himself. So he explained how Tendril had told him he had lost the jade bottle and ran through the people in the Scrum who could easily have taken it. 'How can it be a prank gone wrong' he finished, 'if someone's deliberately trying to put the blame on Tendril?'

'You think young Tendril is telling the truth?'

Seth tried to push away the thought that they had both been doing magic secretly while Calamus was out. And then there had been that woozy, sick feeling that followed. And Calamus saying he'd been with Tendril. And Nightshade accusing him of being drawn to Tendril's potentially dark magic.

'He gets picked on, I think mainly because he got apprenticed to Calamus who is, er, does, er, look a little . . . you seem to know him. Do you think he practises sinister magic?'

A smile played on the inspector's lips and he

poured himself more tea from the penguin pot. 'Another of your good qualities, Seth, is your ability to see the best in people. I find your comments always very insightful.'

'Really? Angelique always tells me I have a terrible habit of trusting all the wrong people.'

Seth found he was longing to talk about this with Angelique. But she was off on her own case. He had vowed not to bother her.

Pewter took a thoughtful sip of tea. 'You are right, even that jade bottle doesn't narrow things down as much as we'd like. Our difficulty is that Leaf's office is more of a draughty corridor, really. People are passing all the time. Something her principal, Haddock Troutbean, finds undignified and complains about frequently. Young Leaf Falling had work she wanted to concentrate on. So Troutbean left her to it – he'd no worries beyond that it can get a little chilly sitting there for too long.'

Seth leant forward, giving Pewter all his attention as he realized the inspector was telling him about the case.

'Leaf looked well snuggled up, wrapped in a pink scarf, he says, and with a glass of milk in front of her. But when he came back, a while after she was supposed to have gone home, she was still there –

that's when he discovered she was in a Deathly Slumber.'

'Was there something in the glass of milk?' Seth poked around for the very last of the fruit at the bottom of the tall glass. 'The day Myrtle was cursed, she had half eaten a strawberry cupcake.'

'The spell was not in the cupcake,' said Pewter. 'And unfortunately the milk had disappeared. But that little jade bottle was discovered on the floor nearby.'

'Well, that could easily have been planted,' said Seth quickly. 'What about the magic – was it the same spell that cursed both of them? That's difficult to tell, right?'

'That is what I mean by you being very insightful, Seth. We don't have that information, because our curse breaker, Finch Charming, is away, sailing single-handed to the Monstrosity Islands, and I am left asking myself several really tricky questions that I can't possibly answer.'

'Two apprentices have been struck down with sinister magic at the same time the Elysee expert is on holiday? That's bad timing.'

Pewter turned his gaze fully on to Seth, those bright blue eyes seeming to bore right into him. 'I very much hope so. Much worse is if it's good timing.'

The inspector's meaning sank in slowly.

'You mean someone knew the curse breaker was on holiday?'

Pewter only raised his eyebrows in response. The moment Seth swallowed the last mouthful of tricker-chockerglory, the inspector scraped back his chair and got to his feet. They said farewell and left Glad to her empty cafe.

Seth fell into step with the inspector as they walked back to the Belle Boutique. 'What do you really think, sir?'

'Think? All I try to do is read and interpret facts correctly.'

'If someone has struck now, knowing the Elysee curse breaker is away, then surely that points to someone who knows about senior Elysee people?' said Seth, thinking aloud. 'There are plenty of powerful sorcerers opposed to how the apprentice scheme is being run. And Myrtle Rust is from a non-magical family.'

They were approaching the pillar-box red of the boutique and Seth knew his chance for asking questions was almost over. Dare he ask if Pewter thought Calamus was behind the attacks?

'If I *was* to think, I'd quite probably end up concluding that the time to be most wary of your enemy is when they are quiet,' said Pewter.

'Quiet, sir? Enemy? What do you mean?'

Even as he said it, something came to mind. Seth knew there was one particularly dangerous sorcerer who troubled MagiCon. Someone who was committed to keeping the world of the sorcerers closed to outsiders from non-magical families. And his followers were growing.

'You don't think Red Valerian is involved?' gasped Seth. Pewter's biggest enemy was known only by this code name. No one knew his real identity. Seth couldn't help it, but he glanced quickly over his shoulder. Red Valerian could be anyone, but wasn't it likely he was based in Gramichee?

'Actually, considering the attacks are on apprentices, one of the most interesting aspects of this case is that I'm pretty sure Red Valerian is not behind it. I'm not sure if that's a good thing.' The inspector put his head on one side. They had stopped outside the Belle Boutique.

Even the thought of Cheery's anger could not stop Seth lingering, hoping for more. Pewter put his hands deep in the pockets of his navy suit. He towered above Seth.

'Red Valerian likes to let us know about his trail of crime and destruction. He likes to make a fanfare so we all run around in a panic. He leaves his calling card. This case bears none of his hallmarks. That only makes me worry what he's plotting next. But I am too busy being perplexed about what is really behind these attacks. A prank gone wrong – isn't that what you said, Seth? Let's hope that's what it is.'

The inspector looked at Seth, his eyes suddenly as blue as little pieces of sky. 'Now, Seth, you can do me two very big favours.'

'Anything, Inspector.'

'I don't like this business of the jade bottle at all. You are in a unique position, Seth, to learn if any of the apprentices truly mean each other any harm. What I would love to do is to eliminate the apprentices from our enquiries. Keep your eyes and ears open, but also look out for yourself – I mean it.'

'Of course.'

But Seth hardly heard the warning. All he cared about was that he was in! Finally he had a part to play in solving the latest MagiCon case.

18. A Sinister Sorcerer in the Making

'Where the fishcakes and salmon have you been? I had to start the clearing up!' Cheery focused another of her scorching looks on Seth. 'You'd better finish before Miss Young gets back or there will be big trouble. Huge.'

Seth thought about trying to edge a sort-of apology into the rapid-fire scolding Cheery specialized in, but Nightshade brushed past his legs. He bent to pick her up.

'So much for my nap,' she mouthed in his ear,

disguising the words as a low purr.

He snuggled into her fur. 'So?'

Cheery put her hands on her hips. 'So, you'd better get on with it!'

'Just heard Calamus say he's off to St Joanne's Walk,' went on Nightshade. 'That's where he said he was yesterday. Wouldn't you like to find out where he's really going and what he's up to, if we're going to save Tendril from being arrested by Dagger Tourmaline?'

Cheery went from attempting to toast Seth around the edges to stunned silence as he edged back out of the door. 'Sorry, Cheery, I actually need to go out again, right now.'

She hadn't yet found her voice when the door closed behind him. He'd deal with her raging later, but for now he followed his cat as she raced ahead, tail in the air. They hurried through the narrow streets of Gramichee, which always twisted unexpectedly, making Seth suspect the streets actually moved.

Luckily, Nightshade seemed to sense where they needed to go, and finally they caught up with a hurrying shape swathed in a full-length cloak with the hood up. The street went into a long curve. It was well-lit, the yellow sodium haze of street lights oozing out on to the narrow pavement. Seth ducked into a doorway, not wanting to risk being seen.

'Watch where you're putting your great feet,' hissed Nightshade.

The buildings were thinning out and they reached a road where street lights petered out completely. This marked the edge of the town. Seth crossed to the other side of the long, straight road, lined with an old stone wall and a grassy verge dotted with ancient trees that would give some cover.

'Think about it, Seth. If Calamus says he was with Vetch, he gives *himself* an alibi, more like.'

'Ah, yes, that's good thinking,' said Seth, keeping watch on the figure ahead and not entirely liking the fact that his cat had reached this conclusion first. 'Where do you think he's going?'

'If I knew that, would I be following a suspected sinister sorcerer creeping around, up to no good and possibly planning to attack another apprentice? Lucky there's a big moon,' said Nightshade, 'or we'd have lost him.'

'Three quarters full,' muttered Seth, taking cover behind a tree.

'I guess that's what you call it when it looks like someone's taken a big slice off one side with a sharp knife? Anyway, what I really want to know is how soon can we leave?' said Nightshade.

'We've come this far, why stop following him now?'

'I don't mean when can we leave this dark and empty street with what looks like a graveyard coming up on our right – it would have to be an overgrown graveyard full of creepy statues when we follow some sinister guy in the moonlight, wouldn't it? No, I mean go back home. It's this place, Gramichee. I told you, it creeps me out.'

'Probably because you're having to work so hard chasing those mice,' said Seth. 'Inspector Pewter has asked for my help.' Then Seth noticed something interesting right by his feet. 'Ooh, mushrooms!'

'Not now, Seth!'

'Just a few. I'm not doing any harm. I guess folk here aren't used to foraging for food,' said Seth, nodding at a cluster of cottages opposite the grave-yard. 'No one seems to want these. Might put them in an omelette. Shame to waste them.'

'Omelette! Whiskers and white mice, Seth, you are not paying attention. This whole place is twisted. We need to leave, and not just because apprentices are being attacked.' Nightshade's big eyes gleamed in the moonlight. 'Even the name, Gramichee: have you worked out that's an anagram of *magic here*? This whole place is trying too hard to not appear what it really is.' She gave a little shiver. 'I don't like anything about being here. Even the mice, Seth, are not natural, and you never offer to help.'

'I'm not sure I'd be much help catching mice. And I do kind of have my mind on other things.'

'Yeah, like doing magic with the prime suspect in a magical crime. What a triumph.'

Seth failed to think up a suitable reply, mostly because it was far from the first time he'd had the suspicion that the only magic he would ever be able to do would be of the wrong sort. But surely that spell he'd done with Vetch had just been a curlotion for sneezing. It had been OK, hadn't it?

'You *would* be rubbish at catching mice, though,' went on Nightshade, nudging Seth. 'But you could at least help by getting that cellar door open. I reckon it's toasty down there by the boiler, and that's where they're all resting their paws. Only I can't get past the door.'

'Nice and warm, heh? I'm sure you're not planning to slip off for a nap, are you, Nightshade?'

'No need to be sarcastic.'

'Angelique's mother arranged for this placement. I have to see out the month.'

Seth looked up at the almost-full moon, thinking of the clock in the shop ticking down to his Prospect. Surely he could learn one decent spell, and one that wasn't going to have him labelled as a sinister sorcerer in the making.

'Least Calamus hasn't spotted us.' Seth said, his pockets now bulging with mushrooms.

'There might be a reason for that. Thanks to your omelette, Seth, we've lost him.'

He peered around the tree at the long, straight road ahead. The cloaked figure was nowhere to be seen.

19. The Wave Glass

'How's it going?' came a voice, very loud and totally disembodied. Seth leapt about a foot in the air.

It was Angelique, and it was just as well they'd lost Calamus, because she was coming through at a volume that would have totally given the game away. Seth saw that one of his pockets was glowing, and pulled out the wave glass Angelique had given him.

The sea-worn, smooth crackled glass looked even more amazing now that the doughnut-like hole in its centre was radiant with a shining light. Seth made the mistake of looking right into it, and was left blinking away shooting stars at the back of his eyes.

'You're really loud and incredibly bright,' he winced.

There was a very familiar Angelique *hrrhmph*, and when he blinked and looked again, he could see her face peering at him with such clarity he feared she would see right over his shoulder, and realize he was lurking at the edge of a darkened graveyard.

'Er – things are going fine,' he answered, hoping the wave glass didn't give her powers to read his mind, as this was such a blatant lie. Seth could see Nightshade's green eyes gleaming accusingly in the moonlight.

He shrugged helplessly at her, thinking of all the things that had gone wrong in the incredibly short time since Angelique had headed off on a new case. Cheery, who was about as friendly as a porcupine. Miss Young, possibly teaching nothing more than fraud. His chance of getting through the Prospect: worse than ever. And the hazardous fact that he might have done magic with his new friend, who was also the chief suspect in an ongoing MagiCon investigation.

'Good to hear,' said Angelique briskly. 'Then

you've got time to come through.'

'Through?'

'Indeed.'

'To where you are? Now?'

'No, next Tuesday, come for tea. I'll bake scones. Yes today!'

'Sounds like Angelique could do with your help,' growled Nightshade. 'And you should tell her all the terrible stuff happening here. She'd want to know.'

'What's that?' Angelique's face grew slightly larger in the hole.

'Just Nightshade being grumpy,' said Seth hastily.

'Cheers,' muttered Nightshade. The cat was looking up and down the street with her big green eyes. 'You go. Tell Angelique everything. I reckon Calamus went into one of those small cottages down that road over there. Or into the huge, overgrown churchyard full of creepy broken statues and graves. Tell you what, have your chat to Angelique, and I'll check out the cute cottages.' She sped off before he could reply.

Tell Angelique everything? He dreaded her getting even a hint of just how bad things were. 'How do I come through?' he said.

'Not now,' she instructed. 'Just be somewhere I can reach you at midnight.'

144

*

The moment Seth heard the clock in the tall tower of St Joanne's striking twelve times from his cupboard bedroom, Angelique's disembodied arm appeared and grabbed his hand. He braced himself for being sucked into a spiralling whirl of a million pieces, but it could not have felt less like travelling by teleport, something he'd done a couple of times now. Instead, he simply stepped through as easily as walking through a door. Somehow, she was standing right in front of him.

'Told you we'd get a good connection,' she smiled.

Her familiar smell of coconut and firecrackers made him feel as if stepping through a magical glass to somewhere he'd never been before was actually like coming home.

'Why doesn't everyone magical travel by wave glass? It's so much better than teleport,' he commented, noting she was wielding a torch, so he could make out little more around them than shadows.

'I'm glad your apprenticeship is going so well you're becoming such an expert on the magical world now, Seth,' she said with a little smile. 'Actually, it's not that easy finding a pair that match so well. I was lucky.'

Through a high window shone the same almost-full moon as he'd seen above the churchyard. That felt pretty strange. But not as weird as discovering, once his eyes had adjusted, that they were in a long, wood-panelled room lined with displays of shining, evil-looking weaponry that would definitely appeal to Cheery. There were even two suits of armour standing guard.

'Are we heading off to a really ancient war?' he asked, looking about in wonder. 'What did I do – travel back in time?'

Angelique turned on her heel and set off down the room, but now Seth was transfixed by the portraits covering every patch of weapon-less wall. They were all of severe-looking folk with expressions almost as disapproving as Cheery's, all with ferocious red hair and fantastic beards, the latter being the only way to tell the women from the men.

Seth went slowly after his friend and paused by a carved wooden plaque. 'This coat of arms has animals fighting on it.' The image seemed familiar somehow. 'And why the lethal swords? I thought your case was in a school – something about a teacher?'

'Of course the coat of arms has rabbits on it, the whole grounds are teeming with the little fluffy creatures. Welcome to Stoney Warren School for Superior Girls.'

Seth sniffed the air and winced at the smell of overcooked carrots, overlaid with the scent of a malodourous floor polish. *Do they feed the rabbits with the carrots, or the rabbits to the girls? Or both?* he wondered.

Angelique was striding towards a door in the corner. There was something different about her. It wasn't her hair – she had the same glossy locks with a red stripe down one side, currently picked out by a helpful moonbeam. She paused at a suit of armour to give a derisive sniff.

'All this medieval fakery – hardly the most inspiring period for girls. Options didn't exactly stretch to knight training. And this school is most definitely about helping girls with their careers.'

Seth looked upwards at the beams of a vaulted ceiling. 'It's very grand.' He took in a tapestry depicting a lurid mob running through a forest. Cowering in a tree was an old woman whose skin was tattooed with stars and planets. 'OK! I get it. This is a school that teaches them to be witches!'

'It most certainly does not.'

'But weren't medieval times when everyone knew about magic?'

'I guess you are referring to herbal healers.' Angelique turned to peer at the tapestry. 'Believe me, the girls are not here to learn magic. Just the opposite. They are here to be reminded that doing magic is not a great idea if you don't want to stand out in a world where no one believes magic exists any more. Come on.'

As she swept onwards, Seth took out his own trusty torch from his tunic. Switching it on, he finally worked out what looked so different about her.

'You're in a school uniform!' He couldn't help a smirk. 'Are you here cleaning?'

That was what Angelique called her special area of work. She went undercover into places with a known magical history, often where a sorcerer was missing or died unexpectedly, and 'cleaned' any remnants of magic that might still lurk. Remaining magic could be dangerous, but especially for those with no idea at all that magic even existed.

Seth wondered aloud whether she was investigating one of those missing sorcerers she specialized in – those with the status of 'Missing Feared Exploded'. MFE was a special status given to those sorcerers whose whereabouts were unknown after a destructive and confusing battle a few years earlier (only ever referred to as the Unpleasant). This had involved an explosion so terrible it was impossible to identify who had died. Establishing what had happened was still ongoing.

Angelique swirled around angrily and placed a finger to her lips. 'Can you please remember I am undercover here. Why do think I'm in this ridiculous uniform? I don't want anyone to know I am investigating anything. Plus –' she puffed out her cheeks – 'I don't want to end up in another detention.'

'You've been in detention?'

She looked younger in her neat navy-plaid skirt and blue blazer with white piping, and Seth was again reminded that she was only a couple of years older than him. With her incredible magic and her job as a secret magical agent, he always thought of her as somehow not only years, but worlds above him.

'The insane idea was for me to pose as one of the pupils,' hissed Angelique, dragging him along and keeping to the shadows. 'After lights out I am not allowed outside my dormitory. Which has made it virtually impossible to investigate anything.'

Seth fought hard against the urge to laugh – the look on her face and the tone of her voice told him it would be a very bad idea.

They reached a heavy wooden door, which Seth now saw was covered with studded ironwork, and slipped quietly through into an entrance hall of polished tiles that swept around an impressive staircase of dark wood. Seth marvelled at the size of the front door as they tiptoed past. 'Wow, could get an elephant in through there.'

Angelique wanted to rush on, but Seth resisted as much as he dared. He wanted to linger and take everything in. The smell here was less carroty, more expensive lavender and beeswax. It was cluttered with less battle-friendly memorabilia, dominated by a tall wooden board with a roll call of previous head girls in gold lettering.

Seth found himself grinning. He suddenly felt incredibly happy to be sneaking around this weird old school with Angelique. 'Do you need my help, then? Must be going badly if you're desperate enough to call me in.'

Angelique surprised him by shaking her head. 'It's not an S3 case. I'm on the trail of a missing teacher, but it's a favour to . . . someone.'

'So, a magical teacher was working here but the school doesn't teach magic? I'm confused.'

'Here's the story: the house belongs to a magical family, but one that gradually lost their magic, and their fortune.' She spoke quietly in his ear, still trying to move him along faster. 'When the inheritance passed to someone who happened to be a teacher, she decided it would be perfect for a small private school. With her magical links, she specializes in helping sorcerers' kids. She teaches them how to fit in with ordinary people – how to do things without magic. Lots of magical families send their children here. Have done for years.'

Seth dawdled by a glass cabinet crammed full of trophies for ordinary things, like tennis and football. Nothing that would give the merest hint that anyone here was magical.

'And the missing teacher? Is she magical?'

Angelique shook her head. 'Elfreda Oldcastle is a relation. From the same family whose magic had dwindled. Devoted her whole life to teaching chemistry.' Angelique crossed to a small door on the other side of the grand staircase. 'Betty thought it was time for Elfreda to retire, but Elfreda wouldn't hear of it. Said the school was her life; been here so long she was as fixed as the wooden panelling.' Angelique pressed her palm flat against the dark, pitted wood of the small door. 'Next thing, she's vanished.'

'Who's Betty?'

'The head.'

Angelique whispered something he couldn't hear. Bolts moved back as silently as if they'd been oiled and the door clicked open with an obedient, smooth silence. *Magic.* Seth wondered if he would ever stop feeling the thrill.

There was little that would distract Seth from watching magic. But something incredible caught his eye. He was peering into a glass-fronted display cabinet crammed with gilt and silver cups in different sizes, all engraved with names and dates of past pupils. He knew the names of quite a few magical families, and was challenging himself to recognize anyone who had sent their children here.

Then one name took him totally by surprise. One of the smallest silver cups, almost lost among the oversized trophies for running, karate and netball, had been awarded for mathematics to a girl called Betony Greenlock.

'Angelique!' He could not speak without his voice shaking as much as the finger he pointed with. 'This cup. Why is my mother's name written on this cup?'

20. A Room Empty of Magic

'Lots of magical families send their children here, like I said. I think even my mother spent time here,' said Angelique. She came back from the door, briefly wrinkled her nose at the tiny trophy and grabbed Seth's arm. 'Come on. I really can't afford to get caught.'

But he didn't want to move. He stared. It had been absolutely the last thing he had been expecting – to be centimetres from something his mother had touched. He looked about with sharpened curiosity.

His mother had been here, had walked in these rooms.

He tried to picture her in a school uniform similar to the one Angelique was wearing. Being presented with that cup. There might be all sorts of clues here that would help him find answers to things he desperately wanted to know about his family.

His eyes locked on that small silver cup. She had been good at maths. That discovery was as good as finding treasure. He knew so little about her.

He resisted Angelique's gentle pressure on his arm. 'She took my father's name when they married and was Betony Seppi. Before that, she was Betony Greenlock.' He wished he could reach his hand through the glass and hold that trophy his mum must once have held. 'And I think she also had some sort of ancient magical name, Wich Wracht.'

Angelique tried once more to gently move him. 'Honestly, Seth, it's not all that surprising that she came here. There are so very few magical folk about, and they very often send their children to places like this – places that are going to understand they are a little different. Now, come on.'

He let himself be dragged through the small door Angelique had unlocked. It opened on to a narrow twisted staircase of polished wood, the smell of beeswax strong again.

'Now, no talking here. We have to go past where teachers are sleeping,' said Angelique, her finger to her lips.

They followed the staircase all the way up to a room lined with more wooden panelling. It made the walls feel closer than they were, even though moon-beams did their best to shine a friendly light through the diamond-shaped panes of ancient windows.

Angelique swung the torch light about, but there didn't seem to be much to look at. A long bench made out of heavy wood. Almost-empty bookshelves stretching from floor to ceiling on two walls. The smell was ancient chalk and dust.

'OK, Seth,' Angelique said quietly. 'What do you make of it?'

It was difficult to make anything of it. He stopped himself saying that it was dark and it was empty. It was tough to concentrate on anything other than his mother. When her whole history was a blank, discovering something about her was a gift. He wanted a moment to savour it. Even more, he wanted a chance to seize this thread and follow it. It might lead to more treasure, more discoveries.

But Angelique had asked for his help and he didn't want to ever let her down. He paced the room softly, trying to wrench his mind into the here and now.

'It's a grand old place.' *Focus.* 'You said magic died out in the family that owned it, and that's why it's now a school? It's huge for a family home. I guess as magic is so rare, many of the old magical families are wealthy?' He paced quietly, but his thoughts were loud. 'I guess that's one reason why so many want to keep sorcerer training for the privileged few. And are not keen to actively recruit people from outside and give those who might have a spark of magic a chance? Their magic could turn out to be strong.'

He saw Angelique was nodding. He looked about the room of this once-magical home, from where magic had disappeared. He thought about those families who discovered their magic was fading, their privilege and influence diminishing. Their once grand houses being turned into schools.

He felt weirdly distracted by the moonbeams, watching how the ancient glass in the windows played with the shafts of moonlight and made them spill into little uneven puddles on the floor and walls. Somehow, the room seemed to smell of moonbeams, as well as the chalk and dust. *Focus.*

Angelique was waiting, but he didn't know for what. She played with the strand of red in her otherwise dark hair. 'Betty's convinced she's coming back.'

He played his own torchlight over a desk, its drawers emptied. He took down one of the abandoned chemistry books. He guessed these abandoned books in this empty room must be all that was left of the missing teacher.

'This doesn't seem the room of someone who's coming back.'

Angelique shook her head. 'I just can't think why she's cleared out so completely. Not when she said this school was her life.'

Seth tried even harder to concentrate. He could think of only one reason Angelique was here. 'Do you think something bad has happened to her? Something magically bad?'

But that still didn't explain why she needed his help. Clearing up bad magic was what Angelique was brilliant at. Although, now he'd been in here a while, there was something . . . a peculiar smell underlying the dust that was niggling at him. A smell so faint as to make him almost think he was imagining it. A smell he'd caught once or twice recently, and he hadn't been able to place it; sweet, citrusy and garlicky all at the same time.

Now he'd caught it, he couldn't stop sniffing. He had a feeling he might be annoying Angelique as he followed his nose. It was only then that he realized something else was very different about her, besides the school uniform. 'You're not carrying your divinoscope.'

She always carried a red lacquered cane with a silver top. It was a magical instrument that helped her check where magic might have been used. She seemed weirdly incomplete without it.

She sighed. 'I couldn't risk being caught using it. Someone had this crazy idea I was perfect to go undercover as a schoolgirl. The plan was the students might have an idea of what happened to the extremely missing Ms Elfreda Oldcastle, and would talk to me. I suppose children often do have a pretty good inkling of what's going on, but I think the girls straight away thought I'm here to spy on them and report if they are doing magic.'

Seth stopped by the big workbench that had been shoved to one side of the room.

'I want to be able to say I've looked into it and there's no evidence anything bad has happened. An elderly teacher decided she'd had enough of teaching and did what Betty has been trying to get her to do for ages – retire and live quietly in the countryside and keep bees.'

'Without telling anyone?' Seth said. 'And why clear out everything? I can see why you're uneasy.'

Angelique sighed. 'The truth is, I'm here as a favour to my mother and I've missed something. I'm not imagining it. There's something here that seems wrong.'

He bent low. The faint smell was coming from beneath the desk, right by where a moonbeam was shining, as if pointing a helpful finger. He felt the underside of the desk and sniffed again. 'Stop looking at me as if I've gone mad.'

'I'm not, I am looking at you in amazement,' replied Angelique. 'Because it took me several hours to find it. You went to it straight away. In this whole room there was only one thing I can identify as magical. Magic is strictly forbidden here, but it's not surprising that some of the students indulge in a little experimentation on the quiet. What I didn't expect was that.'

She pointed at the charred lump Seth found stuck to the underside of the desk, as if it had been spilt and hardened as it dripped. He broke off a piece and stood up. It was blackened, like something left behind after a fire. He put out his tongue and tasted it.

'Ugh! I didn't ask you to eat it. You've no idea what it is! It looks like something left over after you've been practising magic on it, Seth. Any ideas what it might be?'

Seth shook his head.

'I've been able to detect little puddles of mixed-up, amateur magic throughout the school. Exactly the sort you'd expect where magical children are gathered together and banned from doing any magic. But all my instincts are saying there's been illicit experimenting with something stronger. But Betty's like a hawk for spotting magic. If some bad experimentation has been going on, wouldn't she know?'

'I don't know, Angelique.' Seth was still examining the cinder. 'Magic isn't always what people think it's going to be. I had no idea there was magic at the Last Chance Hotel. Things others thought strange did happen, but to us it was just . . . normal.'

'That tiny hardened black lump of cinder is my only evidence. I need to know what it is. What magic has been done here? I can't ask any of the usual Elysee experts, because I'm here unofficially. So I thought of you. Because it has a weird smell.'

'Cheers.' He took the lump and tucked it in one of his many pockets.

'I only meant you're good with your nose. Any chance at all you might have a think about what it is? I'll keep digging here. Because I don't want to go back to my mum on the first case she's ever asked for my help with and tell her I've failed.'

PART THREE

21. Sinful Skin and Delicious Demise

Life was brisk being part of a successful magical business, although Seth's tasks were less magic and more tidying up, plus ringing huge amounts through the till that always tried to snap off his fingers.

He watched the relentless progress of the moon clock. The days were flying by and Miss Young was still too busy to teach them anything. She exhausted herself by visiting sick children at home whenever she could.

The kitchen prep area was constantly messy with measuring jugs, bottles and mixing bowls. It reminded Seth of a chef at the Last Chance Hotel who'd been incapable of making anything without sloshing cake mix and soup broth over every surface, using every single implement and pan in the kitchen and leaving it all for Seth to clear up. He had breathed a huge, though guilty, sigh of relief when the chef's grandmother had been taken ill and the chef had rushed home to look after her, never to return.

He watched as Miss Young once again grabbed her long outdoors coat, slung her stethoscope around her neck and lifted the hood to cover her shining hair. She stirred a generous spoonful of Perfectly Prime Powders into a glass of water and glugged it down.

'And no mixing without me,' Miss Young trilled, wagging a finger. 'Just keep selling, apprentices!'

She might flutter about how all this work was playing havoc with the smooth skin of her hands, but as she rubbed in a little Sinful Skin, Seth would see her do a quick check on the day's takings and saw her secret smile.

'Apprentice and Apprentice Assistant,' corrected Cheery quickly. She slumped in her beanbag once

Miss Young had gone. 'Yeah, cos mixing sticky cream with a glug of overpowering mandarin scent is *soooo* difficult,' she grumbled. 'Like, she needs that elaborate stethoscope and all those fancy extra tubes and everything because she is *definitely* an *actual* doctor.'

As he rolled up his sleeves for more clearing up, Seth considered suggesting he and Cheery risk trying to make up one of Miss Young's preparations without her. If it went well, Miss Young might be pleased, seeing as she was worn out by being busy.

But he was daunted by that complicated spell and incredible list of ingredients for Tendril's curlotion. What chance would they stand of getting something like that right? Would Cheery even help him? And would he ever learn to do a spell like that by himself?

Cheery's mood never rose above sour, fidgeting between the beanbag and staring out into the square, fixing her eyes on the cafe as if expecting another attack. The fact that so many in Gramichee now avoided the Scrum did not stop Cheery meeting Dagger there every chance they got. The MagiCon apprentice had made no arrests over the Deathly Slumbers of Myrtle Rust and Leaf Falling.

As he polished the windows, Seth wondered how he could find out more about the apprentices and truly help Inspector Pewter answer his question about how serious the rivalry between the apprentices was.

The only time Cheery had come even close to friendly had been when he'd prepared himself an omelette with some eggs he found in the cupboard and the mushrooms he'd foraged near the graveyard. Cheery had hovered, eyes following hawk-like as he tested that the eggs were set in the pan, just a little soft, right in the middle, the field mushrooms giving a delicious earthy aroma with a few herbs he'd picked.

Don't do it. Do not give her any. She didn't share so much as a chip with you. Don't say it.

'Would you like some, Cheery?'

She'd grabbed a plate.

He'd divided the omelette in half and they'd eaten together, listening to the hum of the boiler in the cellar that made Seth's store cupboard bedroom so unbearably hot.

'What's this green stuff?' Cheery had asked, poking about as she munched.

'Herbs mostly. And a bit of nettle.'

She'd stopped chewing, eyes accusingly wide. 'You trying to poison me?'

'Nettles are nutritious. And delicious. Bit like spinach. Helps give you strong muscles. I like finding out about plants and stuff and I live in a forest where there are loads of things which are really good to eat.'

'Yeah? Well, there again you are weird. Who actually likes spinach?' But she'd carried on chewing.

'You do have to be a little careful with the stings, though.'

She'd blinked wider and chewed more slowly, but was soon scraping her plate noisily with her fork.

Seth had taken the opportunity to probe with questions about how the other apprentices were getting along. Cheery wouldn't be drawn into saying much, even about what Miss Young was supposed to be teaching.

'Curology. Remedies with added magical value, that's what it's s'posed to be about.' She'd waved her fork at the towering white boxes and licked off the last of the omelette. 'But far as I can see it's all fish-cakes and hokum. I seriously should shop her to Mr Opal for failing to teach any actual magic. It's *my* time she's wasting.'

Was Cheery simply being sour? Or was Miss Young truly never going to teach them anything?

As Seth cleared up between customers now, he knew he had to get Cheery to talk. Did he have time to go foraging and cook something again? That had been the moment she had been the most approachable.

He might feel any chance of getting answers

about the case may have stalled, but at least his confidence dealing with customers was growing. Everyone was friendly and eager to buy, often purchasing the odd healing crystal. Even the dream-catchers with their annoyingly dangling feathers got snapped up, as if Miss Young's magic touched everything, even dreams.

The gentle tinkling of the doorbell and the answering music of the hanging crystals and charms summoned him as Granny Onabutter pottered in. Seth stifled a groan. He'd seen little of her knitting and gossip the last few days, just her pressing her nose against the glass, as if waiting for the shop to be quiet to come in. He had too much to do to listen to her chatter.

'It's only me!' she cried. Seth waited for her to shift the handsome cat and ease herself on to the lips chair, and prepared to be polite through a good half an hour of knitting and clacking. But instead, she shifted her wicker basket to the other arm and said she was simply here to buy more Perfectly Prime Powders.

'No walking stick today?'

'Oh, I don't need it so much, not with this early spring sunshine and having all these young people in Gramichee,' said the old lady, counting out money.

'Or maybe it's because Miss Young is quite the genius.' Her little black eyes lit up. 'She's so quickly become such an important part of this town. So hard-working. Dashing about, looking after everyone. You and Cheery are so lucky! Chosen to learn all her secrets.'

'Go easy on those powders, Granny,' called Cheery as the old lady left. 'It does say only take them once a day. She's getting through them like sweets,' she muttered under her breath to Seth. 'Just as well they don't really do anything.'

But for the first time it struck Seth that Cheery's theory that Miss Young's remedies weren't so very magical might not be correct. Could it be that Miss Young's slowness at teaching them was deliberate, because she wanted to keep the details of her very lucrative magic all to herself?

The front door tinkled just as Cheery headed through to the kitchen, and Seth was surprised to see Tendril walk in. Seth hadn't had a chance to see Tendril, not since the time they'd put that spell together. Seth still wished he could be sure whether he'd done magic then or not. But he'd worried about bothering Ten as Seth had seen Dagger repeatedly at the Curorium and guessed he was still under questioning.

'Sorry I've not invited you back round to try some more magic,' Ten breathed quietly. 'But Calamus has hardly left me on my own. Can't decide if he's worried about these attacks or he just doesn't trust my sorcery's any good. But I've got a curlotion to do. There's been an infestation of sound flies over at one of the schools. Do you want to come over later and give me another hand with my magic?'

Seth couldn't forget that weird woozy feeling he'd had last time he'd helped Tendril with a spell, but he was beginning to despair. Mrs Squerr would expect him to take his Prospect before he'd had a single chance to learn magic with Miss Young. Ten was at least offering him a chance.

Ten looked awkward and shy as Seth hesitated.

Seth found he was smoothing the wave glass in his fingers and could almost hear Angelique's voice saying: '*You do have a habit of trusting the wrong people.*'

'They're just tiny flies you can hardly see,' explained Tendril. 'You know that buzzing you sometimes get in your ear for no reason? Whole school is affected by that.'

'And you need magic to get rid of them?'

Seth remembered Ten's words when they had made that sneezing curlotion. *I think, together, we just did brilliant magic.* Had they? He really needed to find a spell, any spell, he could demonstrate at his Prospect. Time was running out.

Well, he wasn't learning much from Miss Young. He had to decide. Sound flies – it wasn't as if that spell could be used on a person . . .

He gave Tendril a nod and smiled. What harm could it possibly do?

22. Trusting The Wrong People

Cheery had somehow slipped out – Seth could see across the square to where she and Dagger were approaching the fluttering umbrellas of the Scrum.

He was taking one risk by promising to go and learn more from Tendril later. Perhaps he had to take another and find a different way to discover what secrets Dagger and Cheery were sharing.

He glanced at the blue clock. This part of the day was generally the quietest. He had to chance it. He hastily scribbled a sign. *Back in 10 mins.*

Seth kept to the outside of the square, thinking how much easier it would be to listen in on a conversation if your magic was good. Maybe one day he could turn himself into a pigeon, or make his hair long and blond as a disguise. But for now all he could do was pretend to be very interested in the books in a tall rack outside Rook's Storytellers. He could just about watch and listen while keeping himself from being noticed.

He was lucky that today the wind had dropped and Cheery and Dagger had braved a seat outside and their voices carried to him easily.

'Oh, you'd be surprised,' Dagger was saying loftily, taking a spoonful of his favourite trickerchockerglory. 'There are plenty of powerful people against the whole apprentice scheme. This is a serious case I've taken charge of . . . I mean, really serious. But I can't discuss it.'

'Guess your thinking is that it's not an apprentice behind it then?'

'It's a MagiCon case, Cheery, my lips are sealed.'

There was a scraping of a chair. 'If I can't help you, there's no point me watching you eating ice cream.'

In the reflection in the bookshop window, Seth could see Dagger reach out and grab Cheery's hand desperately.

'Please. Things have got really serious, Cheery. You have to help me.' Dagger's handsome face took on an agonized expression. 'I was this close to getting him to confess today. You told me you'd help and I have to break that alibi. Things have gone too far and it's up to me to stop it.'

'Too far? But there's been no attack for a few days now,' yawned Cheery.

'But . . . things have got more deadly serious than you can possibly realize.' Dagger's voice dropped so low it was difficult to hear. 'It's all being kept under wraps in case everyone panics. But I was right from the start when I called him the Apprentice Assassin. You must promise me this goes no further.'

'Yeah, all right.'

'Cheery, there's no chance now of a cure being found for Myrtle Rust.'

'No cure? What do you mean? Surely when Finch Charming returns—'

'No, that's just it, Cheery.' Dagger was sounding increasingly desperate. 'It's too late.'

Seth was listening hard. The Elysee curse breaker was away, but as soon as she returned from her trip a cure would be found, wouldn't it? Surely the spell that had hit Myrtle and Leaf could not be unbreakable.

Cheery must have thought the same, because she

said: 'Too late?'

'That curse she was hit with was strong.' Even Dagger's troubled and solemn face did not prepare Seth for what he said next. 'Myrtle died this morning.'

Seth's own horror at this news was reflected in Cheery's shocked face.

'All right,' she said quietly. 'You can count on me. What do you need me to do?'

Learning the secret news of Myrtle Rust's death made it even more tricky for Seth to decide to keep his appointment with Tendril. He knew Dagger was convinced Ten was the Apprentice Assassin, but surely now the spell had proved fatal it was even less likely that Myrtle's death could be down to anyone inexperienced, like Tendril, practising bad magic.

Seth refused to believe it was Tendril. He also knew he could not put off finding a spell he could perform well any longer. That was what had brought him to Gramichee. Even so, as he crept into the pungently smoky atmosphere of the curorium, he asked himself if he should be there at all.

But Nightshade's clever reasoning drifted back to him. *If Calamus says he was with Vetch, he gives* himself *an alibi.* Tendril could not have cursed Leaf.

Hadn't Inspector Pewter asked for Seth's help in eliminating the apprentices from his enquiries? Surely Calamus was a far more likely suspect than his apprentice.

Ten greeted him with another tea made with fresh herbs grown in the courtyard garden and Seth stopped asking himself if it was a smart move to take another secret lesson in magic. Instead, he reminded himself this was his best chance of learning something before his month's deadline was up, and avoid being slung out of the magical world for ever.

But once he caught the aroma of fragrant bunches of herbs drying on hooks, the whiff of something being brewed up over a flame, he felt he belonged here. The moment Seth cast his eye over the neat array of ingredients Tendril had assembled and the well-thumbed book open at a yellowing page of spidery writing detailing another tantalizing curology spell, his curiosity took over everything and he was lost. These were ingredients he recognized; not vats of sticky cream and bottled scent.

'This just really couldn't be more different to Miss Young's preparation area,' he said.

Tendril barked a short laugh. 'Well, if you listen to Calamus, that's because it's all harmless toiletries you make next door and you could almost put anything in those Perfectly Prime Powders of hers. But are you learning good magic?'

Seth wasn't sure how to reply. 'She's pretty secretive about it, actually.' He changed the subject. 'Are all Dagger Tourmaline's visits here bothering you?'

Tendril shrugged and placed a worn bowl on the workbench. 'He's just doing his job. He has to question everyone. I can handle Tourmaline. He's just desperate to prove himself. I guess we all are.'

Seth had to stop himself from blurting out a warning. Did Ten really not know he was the main suspect? That his jade bottle had been found alongside Leaf?

'You're good at staying calm,' Seth said, thinking back to how Dagger and Leaf had both picked on Ten the very first time he'd seen them. How Seth's anger even watching had turned into a dangerous spurt of flame.

'That curlotion you helped me prepare has worked brilliantly,' said Tendril. 'I've only sneezed once since I've been using that. Thanks, Seth. You want to have a go at this one yourself? You can't do any worse than me. It's just sound flies.'

Seth's throat went dry. 'Try it myself? Really? My own curlotion?' He managed a laugh. 'No bad magic involved?'

'We do cures here, we don't kill anyone!' Ten laughed in reply. 'They're sound flies. Even if you get it wrong, it can't hurt anyone. He just sprays it on wood.'

Tendril suggested they make one each. That way they could both try.

'I think it's fair to warn you, I have tried some simple magic,' said Seth. 'Tried to shut a door. The door blew off its hinges. A friend said start with this easy thing: cast this *sffera*, this basic magical light.'

'Go well?'

'Conjuring a tiny pinprick of magical light? What could go wrong?'

'Another explosion?'

'Burnt my hand and started a fire.'

Tendril puffed out his cheeks. 'I'll go and fetch a bucket of water, just in case.'

It really was just like following a recipe.

Seth read the page through twice. Then he helped Ten gather and measure out every ingredient in a series of bowls in the order he would need them. Soon he was lost in deciphering the spidery writing in a book that looked even older than Calamus.

Seth pictured himself doing each step, quickly getting lost in examining the instructions, how precise they were. Anything he wasn't sure of, he read through again, so that before he even began there was nothing he didn't understand.

The most difficult bit was grinding up the cajeput bark, which came in thin white strips, into the powder that was exactly as described. And the oak apple had to be ground, but to granules, not powder.

'Magic takes a lot of concentration, doesn't it?' said Seth, wiping the sweat from his forehead. It was almost as if he could feel a pull from the book, an invisible energy between him and the recipe as he began, so slowly, so carefully, to construct the curlotion. By the time he was frothing up the ingredients, he'd lost all track of time.

Tendril handed Seth a tiny dark bottle labelled ESSENCE OF WORMWOOD and peered into Seth's large wooden mixing bowl. Seth removed the pipette stopper and added a single drop of the dark, bitter-smelling liquid. The final ingredient.

He scraped everything into an iron pan and heated the mixture to just below boiling point, timing it for exactly seven minutes, wiping his brow again, aware just how hot and stuffy the room had become. There was a stillness, just the soft bubbling of the mixture as it simmered. Seth's vision felt blurry. He was feeling slightly sick and a little giddy and gripped the workbench, anxious not to let on how peculiar he felt.

'Seven minutes, nearly there,' was all he could utter, his throat dry, weakness threatening to overcome him. It took huge effort to remove the liquid from the heat.

He wanted to sleep. He felt himself begin to sway and it seemed like somewhere in the distance he heard Tendril talking.

'Seth, you've done brilliantly!' Tendril's dark eyes were shining.

Had he? It was difficult to take in that he might have finally created a magical remedy without a single flare-up or explosion. Was it possible that for the first time, Seth had actually managed to do magic? A curlotion for sound flies. All he felt was hot and as if everything was happening through a mist.

'You've got an affinity, Seth, for curology.'

Seth looked at his spell, his eyelids heavy. A light smoke haze still came off it as it cooled. But then he compared it against the thick liquid that Tendril had produced – sooty, dark and potent. Tendril's spell was completely unlike the clear, antiseptic-smelling liquid in his own bowl. He knew he'd failed.

The room was so hot and stuffy and he was

desperate to get outside into the fresh air and away from Ten, who was just being kind.

Tendril pushed both bowls away and covered them with a cloth, hiding Seth's disaster spell. As he did so, his arm moved the spellbook and to Seth's eyes, now sleepy and confused, the title of the spell they had just done, which had been hidden before, read as *fleekies*. Not a curlotion for sound flies . . . ?

He fought a wave of nausea washing over him. He could no longer pretend. It felt as if his energy had been wrung out of him. He thought of the two apprentices falling deep, deep asleep. All he could think was that he couldn't fight it any more, this desperate need to close his eyes.

'Seth, you really have done it – done magic! Seth?'

He collapsed on to the floor.

23. THAT ANGRY OLD MAN

Seth had no idea how long he had been out for, but he was awoken by someone pushing a cup of warm liquid into his hands and telling him to drink.

'Don't tell Calamus I gave you this. It's expensive,' grinned Tendril.

Seth took a sip of the liquid, a rich and creamy chocolate with just a hint of cinnamon. From the first sip, he felt better. He sat up and looked into his new friend's dark eyes, feeling embarrassed, and started to apologize.

'Don't worry! For a second there I thought you were another victim of the Apprentice Assassin. But I think it's just that you did magic, Seth. It can knock the wind out of you, especially the first few times. But you are drinking one of Calamus's recovery inventions. He's brilliant, isn't he? You'll feel better in no time. You've got a right affinity for curology, you know. You did brilliant.'

Seth closed his eyes, took another sip. For a moment he was back on a stormy cliff-top, when Angelique had also told him he'd done magic. Then, he'd been among other sorcerers and the mix of magic had been heady and strong. It had been difficult to tell if he'd added even some puny magic to that complex mix. The feeling afterwards had been the same – as if his bones had turned to liquid, his muscles had completely wasted and he would need to hide under a blanket for a week to recover.

As he drained the cup, energy and feeling flowed back into his limbs, and he pondered several things. First that the cool, clear liquid he'd produced didn't look right, so this feeling couldn't be down to him having done magic. So what had made him pass out like that?

Second, when he'd looked at the book, why had the title said 'fleekies' rather than a title relating to sound flies?

But before he could ask Ten any questions there was a crack and a soft thump on a window, loud enough so that the boys' heads jerked around in unison. Something had been thrown directly at the pane. It was lucky the glass hadn't so much as cracked.

Seth rose unsteadily to his feet, but Tendril got there first and crouched so he could peep out without being seen.

'It's Herb Camphor. Throwing stuff. Stones today.' Ten said it in a way that sounded like this happened a lot. 'We should be OK. After the first time Herb lobbed a load of eggs this way, Calamus fixed the windows so they're protected. He's an incredible sorcerer. He's even put a charm on the door so that it's more difficult to open for people who come here with bad intentions. And his affinity isn't even charms.'

'Herb Camphor?' said Seth. 'Isn't he the one who got turned blue? Why is he throwing things at us?' He remembered the rumour that Ten had been responsible.

Vetch gave a sheepish smile. 'Er, well, it's probably because it was me that turned him blue. Well, he played a trick on me first.' He puffed out his cheeks.

Seth didn't like the way his insides reacted. Hadn't Armory Opal said that turning someone

184

blue was skating close to being sinister magic? Almost illegal? How had Tendril learnt that?

All his doubts crowded back in. What were fleekies? Why had his spell looked so different from Ten's? What had just happened? And why did he always feel like his brain ended up in a fog every time he came here?

Something heavier was hurled at the window, and this time there was a sharp crack and then a cry, followed by a commotion in the square.

Seth risked edging his face closer to the window and saw Miss Young crouched next to the same angelic-looking boy with blond curls Seth had seen before. He was sitting on the cobbles, blood leaking from an ugly head wound.

Seth dashed into the street to help, hoping no one was going to throw eggs or rocks at him. He helped Miss Young steer a dazed Herb into the Belle Boutique, where they sat him in the lips chair. Miss Young rummaged angrily among her white boxes, yelling at Cheery for bandages and tossing boxes aside as she delved into her medical bag.

Seth made a big mug of sweet tea for Herb and Miss Young stuck a wad of dressing on his forehead. Herb began to mutter something, but seemed too dazed to even know where he was.

Miss Young fidgeted uncertainly with her stethoscope as if she didn't quite know what to do with it. She looked uneasily at Cheery and Seth and then stuffed it back in her medical bag. Seth didn't miss Cheery rolling her eyes.

'That angry old man, what's he been up to now?' Miss Young snapped.

Seth guessed Miss Young was talking about Calamus, and was about to try to explain about the eggs and mud and stones being thrown at Calamus's shop, and how the curologist had fixed some sort of protective charm on the windows, when Miss Young, her pale skin looking red and angry, revealed she already knew all that.

'I understand he might want to stop people breaking his windows.' She got Herb to hold a wad of tissue against where the blood was still flowing. 'But I know a rebound and redouble curse when I see one.' She looked at the tissue when it came away still bright red. 'I should report him for this.'

'What does . . . a rebound and redouble curse do?' asked Seth.

'It doesn't just stop whatever's been thrown. It goes right back to the thrower and does worse to them than they intended,' said Cheery, passing a fresh bandage.

'That horrible old man,' said Miss Young, wiping away more blood. 'Always sneaking around. I keep hearing someone in the courtyard out back. I'm sure he's spying on us. He just can't stand the competition.'

Seth felt even more troubled. If anyone, it was Tendril, not Calamus, who spent time in the courtyard garden. Why would he be spying? And how had that wicked charm ended up on the windows? Not just one to protect the windows from damage, but a powerful charm that might end in someone being seriously injured.

Uneasily, Seth wandered to look at the charmed windows, thinking about Tendril's confession that he'd been the one to turn Herb blue. That meant for sure Tendril had performed borderline sinister magic. That wasn't good. Obviously Herb shouldn't have thrown a huge rock at the window, but . . .

'The rebound and redouble curse? Is that difficult magic?' asked Seth. He'd asked Inspector Pewter that same question about turning people blue and he'd seemed to think that spell wasn't difficult, just that it wasn't allowed.

'Oh, Calamus could do it with a snap of his fingers,' answered Miss Young.

But it wasn't Calamus Seth was thinking of.

'I cannot stop this bleeding,' tutted Miss Young.

'It's going to be Ward 23 for you, Mr Camphor. Another bed for an apprentice.'

Herb could only groan in reply.

'They'll have to build a Ward 24 just for apprentices at this rate,' said Cheery, hovering until Miss Young shooed her away.

Seth stepped outside to clear his head. A movement at the window next door caught his eye – Tendril Vetch was watching carefully. And his face looked disturbingly and triumphantly gleeful.

Cheery had moved alongside him. She saw that look too, and there was something about the squaring of her jaw that told Seth that if she had any doubts about helping Dagger break Tendril's alibi, surely they had evaporated in that moment.

All over again, Seth remembered how Tendril's arm had nudged the spellbook to reveal they hadn't been working on a curlotion for sound flies at all, but one for something called fleekies. He was positive Ten had deceived him.

It didn't take long for a very short white-coated doctor with a cross red face and a disappointed manner to arrive via teleport to take away the wounded Camphor. Seth and Cheery showed him inside the boutique, but Cheery immediately moved to the window and stayed there, watching.

'D'you think an apprentice would have the power to charm those windows?' Cheery asked Miss Young, who gave her an openly curious look.

Seth waited for her reply. He was just as keen to know the answer to exactly that question.

'An apprentice, Cheery? Perform a charm with one aim in mind – to hurt someone? I seriously hope not. What makes you say that?'

'I don't . . . Just – oh, it's nothing.'

Pewter had asked Seth to consider if any of the apprentices seriously meant each other any harm.

A deeply unsettling feeling churned in Seth's stomach and he felt sick. Could it really be that Tendril Vetch was behind all the attacks? But he'd just helped Tendril with a spell.

An anxious frown settled on Miss Young's face. 'I'm not sure exactly the level of magical ability you'd need to charm those windows. But I'm beginning to think we should ask your MagiCon friend, Dagger Tourmaline, to look into it.' She wandered to look out on to the Forum. 'If that was an apprentice's spell we saw, then it's not how advanced it is that concerns me. It's the very worrying direction it's taken. And that is very worrying indeed.'

24. The Magicon Apprentice

Seth focused on scouring an evil-smelling and weirdly pink-tinged blob that had solidified on the edge of the biggest mixing bowl. He was weary of how much the mess piled up, no matter how hard he scrubbed and tidied between dashing to serve customers.

Keeping up his welcoming smile was becoming even more difficult, as he was so haunted by that vision of Tendril's triumphant face.

He swept the floor so vigorously that Cheery,

huddled in her beanbag, coughed and complained, so he went back to the prep room. He was having as much difficulty shifting the unease in his insides as he was shifting that hardened globule on the mixing bowl.

All day he asked himself the same questions he'd been asking himself the previous night, as he'd rolled in his uncomfortable hammock in his sweaty cupboard, fighting the thoughts roaming his head.

Calamus was surely the best suspect. Calamus had lied about where he was when Leaf was attacked. He was the most skilled sorcerer. Even an apprentice making experimental mistakes with banned magic couldn't accidentally conjure magic that would kill anyone.

Was it Tendril's fault that Herb Camphor had been injured?

Of course Tendril wasn't responsible for the attack on Myrtle – that was serious magic – but had Seth been tricked into helping Ten prepare a sinister spell? No, it was just a spell for sound flies.

Tendril had told him he'd done it well. Tendril had said he had an affinity for curology. Finally, Seth might be getting close to finding something to demonstrate at his Prospect . . . as long as Vetch was telling the truth.

He scrubbed so vigorously the crusted blob finally flew across the room, attaching itself to the wall. He had to dampen down his anger. He'd set light to something more than once when he'd let his emotions get the better of him.

When Dagger came out of the curorium again, swaggering from a fresh round of bullying, Cheery glared at Seth as she passed him on her way out. She fell into step with the MagiCon apprentice, his sleek dark head bent against her aubergine one, and instantly they were deep in urgent conversation. Seth longed to find out where Dagger was with his investigation. The shop was quiet. Could he close for a few minutes?

A sinewy black shape slinked up to him.

'Nightshade! Mice under control yet? Getting any help from Gorgeous Tom?'

'That vain and useless beast? You running this business on your own again, Seth?' Nightshade looked up at him with her big green eyes. 'Hope you haven't forgotten about getting that cellar door open? I'm sure that's where about a dozen of the little furry nuisances have made a snug nest I'd like to terrify them out of. I swear, as soon as I get one there are two more in its place.'

'Yeah, haven't forgotten about that,' Seth lied.

Mice were the very least of his problems. 'Fancy taking a break from the mouse hunt and giving me a hand?'

'I am not getting my fur wet helping you do the washing-up.'

Seth swooped to pick her up, tickled her under her chin and headed back to the kitchen prep room. Hearing Nightshade purr made a welcome change from listening to Cheery's grumbling. Or the painful rumbling of his own brain failing to make sense of anything.

'I want to listen in on what Cheery and Dagger are saying. Perhaps you could—'

Nightshade wriggled out of his arms. 'Isn't there some magic you could be practising? Something useful? Because all I ever see you do is clearing up,' she said, parking her bottom on the countertop. 'Or trying to listen in on Cheery and Dagger, or sneaking next door to learn suspicious magic from that dubious boy. Trust you to pal up with the one with the dark power and the most likely suspect for being behind these attacks,' she said. 'Didn't someone once point out that you always trust the wrong people? And time's running out.'

'Well, not everything points towards Tendril Vetch,' argued Seth, wishing he fully believed it himself. 'Dagger's so keen to make a name for himself with his *Case of the Apprentice Assassin*. He struts around, desperate to get anything he can make stick. He's determined to make an arrest. He'd plant that jade bottle himself if he had to.'

'Oh!' Nightshade paused in polishing her whiskers. 'That's clever. You think he's the one? He was in the cafe when Myrtle was attacked. You reckon he's set a trail of destruction just so he can clear up the case? And he had Ten figured to take the blame from the start, because everyone already thought he was a bad 'un. Good thinking, Seth. He's cunning.'

'That's ridiculous, Nightshade.'

But even as he said it, his mind was asking, *Is it ridiculous?*

Dagger's magic must be already at an impressive level if he'd been offered the MagiCon apprenticeship. Could he have achieved the level of magic needed to put that curse on Leaf and Myrtle? Because Nightshade was right; no one would ever suspect him.

Was that why he'd sounded so shocked about Myrtle's death?

Perhaps he really hadn't meant that to happen. Seth knew better than most how often magic went wrong.

'Better than it being your new best mate?' put in Nightshade quietly.

And she was right. Did he really have a new main suspect? And did it explain everything if it was the MagiCon apprentice himself who was the Apprentice Assassin?

25. A Three-Shortbread Problem

Cheery still hadn't returned and Seth began closing up, his mind still whirring. When he heard the charms above the door go into an attention-grabbing frenzy, he groaned inwardly and turned to serve his last customer, only to discover Inspector Pewter brushing away a green feather dangling from a dreamcatcher. 'Got a moment, Seth?'

'Just about to make tea, Inspector, take a seat.'

'That would be an even grander offer if you told me there'd be shortbread to go with it. But I bet you're too busy polishing your magic for old skills like cooking.'

Every time anyone mentioned Seth's magical progress it was as if a small creature awoke and started scrabbling in his stomach. He unconsciously glanced at the progress of the moon on the blue clock. Tonight it had reached a full moon.

Pewter lowered himself into the red-lips chair and his face took on the perturbed expression of someone who'd discovered they had just accidentally sat on a cat they thought was a cushion.

Seth shooed Gorgeous Tom out of the door.

'Got any good news, Inspector?' Seth asked hopefully as he handed Pewter a large mug of hot tea a few moments later. 'Is this still a three-shortbread problem?'

Unusually, not even the ghost of a smile appeared on the inspector's face. He simply sat there blowing on his tea.

Seth looked at the inspector's face, heavy with concern, and all he wanted to do was to help. Pewter had never been anything less than kind to him. He'd asked Seth to get the lowdown on how serious the rivalry was between the apprentices and now Seth felt bad about how little he'd found out.

'I am here to ask an enormous favour, Seth,'

Pewter said, his as voice serious as Seth had ever heard it.

'Anything, Inspector.'

'I want you to go back to the Last Chance Hotel.'

Seth was shocked. This was not what he'd been expecting. Did the inspector somehow know Seth had been practising magic with Ten? He bet the inspector would know what a 'fleekies' spell was, but he daren't ask.

'You think I'm going to do bad magic?' whispered Seth.

Pewter raised his bushy silvery eyebrows. 'I meant that I do not want my mistakes to put you in danger.'

Seth felt the biggest dangers he faced were his deadline, and failing his Prospect. And possibly what might happen if anyone found out he'd been tricked into doing some bad magic.

You could say things were going so wrong that returning home before he disgraced himself might not be a bad idea. Yet he knew he didn't want to go. Not while he still had a chance. If he could just work out for sure who was the Apprentice Assassin then at least he would know whether he could trust Tendril and any magic they did together.

He distracted himself by tidying the towers of white boxes. 'Put me in danger? You don't have to worry about me as, luckily, I'm not even a real apprentice.'

The inspector shifted in the lips chair, reached into his pocket and handed Seth a small package wrapped in white paper. Slightly squashed.

Seth opened it and the heavenly smell of a crisp ham and cheese toastie filled his nostrils, making his mouth water. 'Thank you.'

'You're welcome – I would have invited you to the Scrum, but they were closing early today due to an unfortunate lack of customers. Never thought I'd see that day in Gramichee. Things could not be more serious, Seth.'

Seth nibbled a corner of the toastie and thought how he wasn't the only one with problems. 'Myrtle dying is horrible. I guess it means people don't want to take the risk of eating in the Scrum. Not until this is all cleared up.'

Pewter sipped his tea slowly. 'Die? There's me, wondering how to break bad news and there you are again – in possession of knowledge that should be top secret.' He uncrossed his long legs. 'Now, I didn't mean to interrupt whatever you should be doing. Anything I can help with?'

What Seth really wanted help with was under-standing the magic he'd done with Tendril, or with putting together any sort of decent spell. Or help in breaking it to the inspector how he had reached the conclusion that the MagiCon apprentice should really be considered a prime suspect.

'It's closing time,' he shrugged. 'So I'm just doing what I always seem to end up doing. Clearing up.'

'Clearing up sounds like something I can easily help with.' Pewter put his head on one side and finally there was that reassuring smile Seth relied on. 'Sometimes, being a detective is just about clearing up. Perhaps it's something we're both good at.'

So the two headed to the prep area to face the remains of the washing-up together.

They worked in silence for a while, Seth trying to align all his tumultuous thoughts. There was so much he wanted to discuss, but he was making a mess of it because there was also much he didn't want to admit to.

Pewter would hardly stay here for hours, helping with the cleaning. Yet how could he share what he'd just discussed with Nightshade – their conclusion that Dagger Tourmaline had a motive for the attacks on the apprentices? And that he could have planted the jade bottle himself.

The Inspector washed bowls and stacked them neatly on the draining board and it was he who finally broke the silence.

'There is no need for you to stay, Seth. If things go on like this, soon there won't be any apprentice scheme for you to join once you've come out the other side of your Prospect. And it was my mistake when I asked you to get involved in the case. A mistake at least I have a chance of putting right.'

'But I can't leave, because . . .' Seth would have loved to disclose that he wasn't learning magic from Miss Young, poured out all his worries about what Ten might have tricked him into and talked through all his troubles. But those were his problems. None of it was the inspector's fault and the inspector had plenty to deal with.

Inspector Pewter's eyes shone blue as he looked at Seth and waited.

'. . . because I haven't seen my mother.'

It just popped out, but once it had, Seth was surprised at how much this had also been worrying at the back of his mind, crowded out by everything else.

'I thought coming here I'd be near her, but where even is Ward 23? No one tells me anything! If I leave, I've no chance of seeing her.' He hadn't meant it to come out so angrily. But it was true – if he had to turn his back on the magical world, what would happen to her?

'People who have been under prolonged magical attack are . . .' The inspector trailed off, and focused on stacking bowls as if it required deep concentration. 'She's not . . . peaceful,' he floundered. 'That will take time. What can I tell you? It's no secret that Ward 23 can only be reached by a portal. It's part of a regular hospital of the non-magical kind. Magical people need regular medical care as well as any other. But I'll ask if there's any way—'

'Sorry. I know you've many more important things to worry about.'

The inspector folded the dishcloth. Seth knew he was about to leave and he hadn't even asked about the rivalry between the apprentices, as if he'd known Seth wouldn't have found out anything useful.

'You asked me to look into what's going on with the apprentices.' Seth found himself speaking quickly, before he lost his chance or his courage. 'Well, I can report that some apprenticeships are definitely seen as better than others and there is some serious rivalry. I know the pranks have got out of hand.' He was remembering Herb Camphor throwing rocks and his head wound. Was that a prank? Then things really had got serious. 'But this sinister Deathly Slumber spell that's been used – everyone's saying that can't possibly be the work of a beginner.'

Seth knew he was desperate for it not to be Tendril, not to have made that mistake. He looked at Pewter, but his expression behind his little round glasses was difficult to read.

'And I keep thinking . . . I keep thinking,' Seth went on, 'well, why did you put Dagger in charge of the case?' The words were out before he knew it. 'There's something between you and Calamus, isn't there? Calamus has to be a suspect. But Dagger's determined to pin everything on Tendril. I can't help thinking he'd do anything to make a name for himself. Even—'

'You think the detective I've assigned to solve the case is the person behind it?' said Inspector Pewter mildly.

Why did this happen when he talked to Pewter? Why did the thoughts he was so determined to keep to himself suddenly get out there?

Pewter tidied away the endless bowls and spoons. 'Your instincts are right. Calamus and I have a history,' he said carefully, as if choosing which of Seth's accusations to answer. 'I was the one who pulled him from the explosion that gave him those burns. I can never work out if he blames me for not being there sooner – or for knowing he'd be there at all.'

Seth took this in. Calamus had been involved in

an explosion – somewhere he shouldn't have been. It didn't sound quite like a magical experiment gone wrong as Seth had suspected. It sounded more like...

'Calamus was involved in the Unpleasant?'

The inspector gave a short nod.

Then surely Calamus had to be the best suspect for being behind it all. But how could they prove it?

'To cure this Deathly Slumber curse, you need to know exactly what magic was in it?' said Seth carefully. 'That's how magic works, right? If you could find the source, that would be a big help in solving the case. You'd be closer to an answer. But your curse breaker, Finch Charming, is away?'

The inspector nodded once more. 'And the only other person whose opinion and expertise I'd trust is someone who, sadly, we can't ask.'

It took no time to work this out. It was obvious to Seth who he meant, even so he asked in surprise: 'You'd ask Calamus?' Did this mean the inspector didn't really suspect the curologist at all? Seth felt a headache starting behind his eyes.

'I would, yes. Unfortunately, to do so would leave ourselves open to the accusation of involving a suspect in the investigation. That never ends well.'

'How about asking Angelique?' Seth hit on the

suggestion brightly. 'She's great on tracking down sources of magic.'

'You'd advise bringing back the daughter of my new boss when she's just despatched her on a case?' Inspector Pewter's eyes gleamed behind his glasses. 'Hmm. My priority is making sure no one else dies – and that includes you, Seth. I promise I'll think about your advice as long as you think about mine.'

But Seth already knew his answer. He had to see this through.

The inspector departed with a promise he'd see if Seth could visit Ward 23.

'There are things even more important than learning, magic, Seth,' said Pewter very quietly as he left.

As he shut the door, Seth at least felt confident that the inspector had no need to worry about him being attacked – that really was one advantage of not being a proper apprentice. He stood looking out of the window for a moment, pondering his next move. But it was suddenly decided for him.

A hand gripped his throat. He felt pressure, started to choke and was hurled backwards into a pile of white boxes as if he was no heavier than a bundle of rags.

26. Top Three on My Suspect List

'What secrets have you been keeping from me?' bellowed Cheery. She applied pressure on his neck with her left arm. 'If you're a MagiCon spy, you'll be toast.'

Seth was seeing stars. His arms flailed, but Cheery was too strong and too practised. His only chance was to talk his way out, and talking was tough when someone was crushing your throat.

His arms thrashed, his fingers reaching for a weapon, any weapon. They closed around a tube of

Delicious Demise, which was far less useful than its name suggested. He smacked her in the side of the head with it and pushed her off enough to wriggle out the words: 'You're choking me.'

'I'm applying a tiny bit of pressure and asking you what the fishcakes you think you're up to. What were you talking about with Inspector Pewter?'

'If you let me go, Cheery, I might tell you.'

Cheery's face still looked ferocious, but she loosened her grip.

Seth staggered upright. 'You've got it all wrong. Inspector Pewter is just a friend.'

'Huh!' she responded, tapping an aubergine-coloured boot furiously on the floor. 'Lies! No one is *just a friend* with someone as amazingly magical and powerful as Inspector Pewter. Especially some turnip who hasn't even passed his Prospect yet. Tell me the truth or—'

'Or what – you'll break my arm?' She moved forward and Seth took a step back, scattering more white boxes as he rubbed his throat, croaking to speak. 'If you didn't spend all your time being nasty and attacking people, I might even tell you. We could have been friends.'

'With you? The person who is trying to steal this apprenticeship off me? And what are you up to now? Stealing any chance of me getting a MagiCon one next year.'

'Believe me, Cheery, this has nothing to do with you.'

Seth started to reassemble the boxes in some sort of order, trying to disguise that his hands were shaking. What hurt more than anything was how Cheery had managed to lurk and listen without him twigging she was there. He didn't like having the tables turned on him, rubbing his nose in how much he was a failure as a detective.

'The only person you are nice to is Dagger,' he went on crossly. 'And that's only because you're trying to get something out of him. Well, you want information from me – you trade. You want to trade – play nice. You are never going to get the MagiCon apprenticeship if you think the way to get information from people is to beat them up.'

'But you're lying – I heard you discussing the case. Pewter isn't just some mate.'

'You think I'm going to share anything with you? I've kept my part of the bargain, I've done all your work so you can go cosying up to your best friend, Dagger, who is seriously up to no good. I didn't ask to work here, but I couldn't say no. All you've done is play tricks on me. It's not as if you want this apprenticeship anyway.'

'What did you say about Dagger?' asked Cheery, her tapping boot suddenly stilled. 'I knew it! You were talking about this case with Inspector Pewter!' Her fury melted into a puzzled frown. 'And what tricks have I played?'

Seth abruptly headed for the door. 'Sending me next door with that dodgy list of sinister ingredients on my first day. You thought you were being so clever.'

Cheery frowned. 'I never did that. Why did you think I did that? All right, I was nasty to you – OK.' She put up her hands. 'Where are you going?'

'For a walk. I need to get out for a bit.'

'I'll come.'

It was on the tip of Seth's tongue to tell her that she was the main reason he needed to get out, but as he'd spent the last few minutes telling her to be more friendly, this hardly seemed a good response. So he shrugged, and held the door open for her.

Cheery fell in alongside Seth as he retraced the steps he'd taken with Nightshade a few nights earlier, threading his way through the narrow twisting streets, heading for the big churchyard. He wanted to do what he always did when he got stressed. Get cooking.

'I'm going to pick some more mushrooms and

herbs. I'm hungry.'

'Pick 'em? That where you got those mushrooms from? Aren't they poisonous?'

Seth sighed, trying to loosen his own anger. 'I know what I'm doing. I've lived my whole life in a wood. Hardly any mushrooms appear at this time of year.'

'Mushrooms.' Cheery unexpectedly chuckled. 'Reckon there'll be enough for two? I'm always hungry. You can make us another omelette. Miss Young's idea of a nourishing meal is a cut-up apple. Expect that's why I'm so grumpy. Are we having nettles again? And you gotta tell me what you got on Dagger. You've got to,' she added as he hesitated.

Seth was trying to decide how much he could trust her, when he saw something that helped to make up his mind. He gripped Cheery's arm. 'Actually, we might also be following Calamus.'

'OK, care to share why?' asked Cheery, as they slid in behind the hooded figure Seth had spotted ahead.

Seth hesitated. The hooded figure was moving quickly and this time Seth was determined to find out exactly where Calamus went – not to visit those twins, Seth felt sure. But he was running out of time and was beginning to think the only way the apprentices were going to stop these attacks was to put all their cut-throat rivalry behind them. And Cheery was smart. And desperate to solve this case.

'He told Tendril he's been visiting those twins with fever, but—' he began carefully.

'But they're Miss Young's patients, gotcha. Any other reasons we suspect Calamus of being up to no good?' quizzed Cheery. 'Apart from the obvious that it's a really powerful spell that was used on Myrtle and Leaf and our neighbourhood curologist is one of the few sorcerers with the skills to conjure it. Is that what Pewter thinks?'

Seth had to make a decision. Could he trust Cheery?

'Calamus is probably top three on my suspect list,' said Seth, remaining evasive about the fact the inspector trusted the curologist and it was his own ideas he was following.

'Three? Who are the other two on the top of your suspect Christmas tree?'

'Well. I know all about MagiCon finding the jade bottle,' he said quietly, making his decision. 'And I know you know about it too.'

Seth hoped he made it sound as if somehow it was all part of some plan that she had been allowed to find out about this critical clue. It was better than admitting just how much he'd learnt from eaves-dropping on her and Dagger so often.

'I knew it! I knew it – you're a MagiCon spy working with Inspector Pewter. Now, tell me everything you know.'

Seth gestured at her for quiet as they headed on carefully after the cloaked figure, keeping their distance.

It would have been pleasant to pretend it was the truth that Pewter trusted him completely and that they were working closely together.

'I don't know as much as you think,' he replied evasively. 'But I do know that Ten says he lost that bottle. Does that mean someone took it deliberately to shift the blame on to him? I also know he had a sneezing attack just at the time Myrtle was found at the Scrum. Someone could have swiped it easily in the confusion.'

'That's interesting thinking, Seth,' said Cheery in a low voice as they carried on, keeping in the shadows. 'Who was in the Scrum around the time Myrtle was attacked? And are any of them likely to have the skills to do that spell? Who are your other two top suspects?'

Seth took a final moment to make up his mind about sharing, before whispering: 'Dagger Tourmaline and Armory Opal.'

27. The Overgrown Graveyard

Seth waited, expecting her to stick up for Dagger.

Unexpectedly, she chuckled. 'I like the idea of Opal. Perhaps he's trying to get the number of apprentices down – less work to do? It's you arriving, Seth. One apprentice too many, so he had to get rid of a couple. And that's what you mean by Dagger being up to no good? You've got him down as a suspect!'

'For anyone wanting to ruin the apprentice scheme, Armory Opal is in the perfect position to do it. He's more likely than an apprentice to have the knowledge to cast the Deathly Slumber spell. But I'm not completely sure Ten is in the clear,' admitted Seth.

'OK. Let's call it a top four, because Calamus could have swiped that bottle any time. But if you think someone seized that moment in the Scrum, you've got to include Glad Tidings.'

They carried on, careful not to get too close to the hooded figure, and agreed Glad was difficult. Glad's business was suffering because of the attack at the Scrum – what might be her motive? But they agreed she should be number five on the suspect list.

Soon they reached the edge of Gramichee – that lonely stretch where everything seemed darker and more menacing as they were no longer surrounded by houses spilling out homely light. In a minute, they'd see the church appear, its tall spire looming threateningly.

'Yeah, I always wondered at Dagger focusing so much on Tendril,' said Cheery, after Seth had shared more of his reasoning. 'P'raps he thought he might be the easiest one to pin the blame on. But we don't have enough to prove it's any of them.'

In the end, Seth didn't bother to collect mushrooms. He didn't want to lose Calamus this time.

This might be their best chance to find out where he really went. He was making his way purposefully towards the vast graveyard, and creaked open an old iron gate in among railings.

'I knew he wasn't visiting those twins,' said Seth as he and Cheery paused by a huge sign reading *St Joanne's*, and listing the times of services.

'Are we following him into the graveyard?' Cheery didn't sound at all keen.

It seemed a pretty mean thought, but Seth was quite pleased that someone as intimidating as Cheery sounded scared, as she was pretty terrifying herself.

'I think we should see for ourselves what he's really up to,' Seth insisted, his voice a whisper.

'St Joanne's,' said Cheery. 'Magical people believe she looks out for them. Let's hope she's looking after us right now. What's old Calamus doing out here in the gloom? Let's hope he's not leading some pagan ceremony to conjure up dark magic. If he is, let's hope he's not bringing a load of mates.'

As they approached the gate, Seth was aware of how loudly it had creaked when Calamus opened it, and was uncertain about how to get through without alerting the curologist that he was being followed. Nightshade would have slipped through easily, and he wished Angelique was here – she'd probably know a silencing spell. He had to be content with opening the gate really slowly.

'Have we lost him?' hissed Cheery, squeezing through after him.

The moon was already a big disc, silvery and low in the sky, showing a graveyard that stretched on and on. Here, near the church, the oldest gravestones were weathered and crowded in untidily. But at a distance the tombstones were arranged more neatly in rows. But the figure had disappeared into the shadowed side of the church and they crept after him.

What was most disturbing about the graveyard was the statues. Dozens of them guarding graves and memorials. Chipped and eroded. An angel, half-broken wings spread out, the lower part of its head bowed in prayer and stumps where clasped hands should have been.

'This is wicked creepy,' breathed Cheery. 'If one of them moves, I'm outta here.'

'Cheery, if one of them moves, I think we're both getting out of here.'

Even if you had complete faith that there was no such thing as ghosts, you'd have to be pretty brave to stride through there as confidently as Calamus was doing. Cheery was hanging on to Seth's arm, her grip tightening every time there was the slightest scuffling of small creatures or wind rustling the overgrown grass.

'It's a full moon,' she quavered. 'That's when dark souls rise from their resting place. And werewolves. Just as well I'm not superstitious.'

'Werewolves are not real,' said Seth uncertainly, hoping this wasn't an unwelcome part of the magical world he was about to be introduced to.

They stayed in the shadow of the church, edging slowly along the rough stone walls. Grass and nettles dragged at their feet. He felt Cheery flinch as something stirred ahead. Then a white shape flitted soundlessly in front of them.

'What was that? Oh fishcakes, that was a ghost!'

'It was an owl, Cheery.'

They hunkered down behind a large tomb and watched the hooded figure bend low, looking much stiffer than when he'd moved through the town.

'OK, so you spend all your spare time foraging in some forest,' Cheery said. 'Is there some weird reason he's waited until it's dark to pick plants?'

Cheery was absolutely right. He was definitely gathering plants and putting them under his cloak.

'An old churchyard like this is going to be fertile

ground for all sorts of ingredients,' Seth said thoughtfully. 'In a wild patch like this, who knows what might be pushing up among the daisies.'

'Ugh! You are joking. You didn't pick those mushrooms I ate from some grave, did you?'

Seth couldn't resist a smile and carried on watching. 'I'd like to know what he's gathering.'

Cheery sighed. 'Here was me hoping you'd say we've hung around here too long already and should really go somewhere with more chance of tea and cake.'

But Seth was lost in thought. 'There are certain herbs that people believe have much stronger medicinal properties if you gather them in the moonlight. And there are some that are at their most powerful at full moon.' Seth looked upwards. 'That's tonight.'

'OK, so he's collecting supplies. Does that mean we can go now?'

The realization that Calamus wasn't attacking anyone or meeting anyone gave Seth the courage to sneak in a little closer. What was the curologist after?

He dared to creep closer towards the figure lifting plants from the ground, close enough to see that the moonlight was picking out the plants, making them reflect with a sort of pinkish luminous light.

'What the hell is he collecting?' asked Cheery. 'You're the expert.'

Seth shook his head. 'I have no idea. But I would love to know, because I have never seen them before in my life.'

28. NOT A SINGLE BIT OF MAGIC

'Could someone *please* help me find another six boxes of my Perfectly Prime Powders before I am even later,' cried Miss Young, rummaging frantically through one of the cupboards that Seth had neatly organized. Several times.

Cheery had already got an earful for being too slow to the market in the Forum that morning to buy supplies. With Miss Young's products being so popular, they were low on everything. Cheery was in a full-on grouch again today, showing no signs of repeating the fragile camaraderie they had achieved in the graveyard the previous evening.

They'd talked more on the way back and Cheery had completely denied that trick where she'd sent him next door with a list of dodgy ingredients. She could just about remember a list with naja berries on it, she said, but couldn't even be sure if the list had been given to her by Miss Young. But she was adamant she hadn't written it.

Seth checked the blue moon clock. He had been waiting nervously all morning for Miss Young to leave, hoping he could persuade Cheery it was essential for him to go next door and talk to Tendril. But every time he looked at that clock, all it did was give him another uncomfortable nudge of how soon his Prospect was looming and that another day would quickly pass during which he'd been far more concerned about the Apprentice Assassin than with his magic. But what could he do?

'Dagger's not showed up today,' said Seth, peering at the curorium next door. He couldn't believe the MagiCon apprentice had finally decided to leave Ten alone.

Cheery shrugged. 'May have gone to the library. He talked about finding a spell someone of Tendril's ability might have used on Leaf and Myrtle. Do you really think it's all a pretence and he's the one behind all this?'

Seth thought with longing about passing his Prospect and being awarded the privilege of being able to visit that magnificent library again.

The library was how sorcerers studied to improve their magic. Angelique had called a library card the doorway to magic. He'd snuck in once on her card. The library was a vast, seemingly endless peaceful space, with an arched ceiling, shafts of daylight that highlighted ancient maps and globes, and shelves and shelves of magical books, towering upwards. But without his own library card – that small, yet precious device awarded to those who passed the Prospect – he had no chance of returning.

And to Seth it meant so much more. It promised the chance for him to fulfil all of his ambitions – to become a great sorcerer and to find out everything he could about his family.

The faint jingling of the bell and the waft of a gentle breeze through the tinkling crystals announced the arrival of Granny and whispered to Seth that, once again, he would get no further towards fulfilling those cherished dreams today.

Granny went straight to the basket of amber

amulets labelled PROTECT YOUR LOVED ONES AND SURVIVE and started rootling through to find the most attractive one.

'I absolutely need one of these for my grand-daughter. Don't want any harm to come to her, not when she starts her apprenticeship. Did you see the *Banshee* this morning? It's calling for the end of the apprentice scheme. It's this news about Herb Camphor.'

'The *Banshee*?' asked Seth.

'Magical morning newspaper.' Granny Onabutter's face creased into papery lines as she smiled. 'You lovely young folk, all so new to the ways of Gramichee.'

As she paid for the amulet, Cheery's face loomed in closer.

'But MagiCon will get to the bottom of the attacks. And Herb Camphor was different. The *Banshee* can't seriously be calling for an end to the whole scheme.'

'Apprentice scheme at an end? Never!' Mr Opal had arrived, bringing a blustery but unconvincing attempt at cheeriness. The drooping bat wings of his hair told the real story.

'If you've come to check on everyone, there's not many left to check up on,' said Granny.

Opal gave her a withering look and wiped a sheen of sweat from his forehead. 'I need a chat with Miss Young.'

'She's late for her medical emergencies,' said Cheery.

The sly look that passed between Mr Opal and Cheery told Seth that Cheery had done what she'd threatened – dropped hints to the Apprentice Finder that Miss Young's magic was – what had she called it? – all fishcakes and hokum. And that their magical tuition hadn't even begun. More trouble for Mr Opal.

But before he started to feel sorry for him, Seth reminded himself that Mr Opal was someone who'd had the chance to swipe the jade bottle. He was also trusted by all the apprentices and he could speak to them any time.

'How many apprentices are you responsible for in Gramichee?' he found himself asking.

Mr Opal looked at Seth through a narrowed gaze. 'How many? Well, one more than I expected. You are still here, young man?'

Ah yes. He had never quite got the chance to explain to Mr Opal why he was here, but he assumed, because Kalinder Squerr had arranged things, that the Apprentice Finder probably knew.

Seth doubted Mr Opal liked a sort-of apprentice being brought in by another senior Elysee official without his say-so. 'Er...'

Cheery only made things worse. 'Perhaps Mr Opal has noticed that these bad attacks pretty much happened the minute you showed up, Seth.'

'It really is not a joking matter,' Mr Opal reprimanded Cheery, two high spots of colour appearing in his pale, paunchy face. 'If Miss Young is busy, I shall check on Mr Vetch next door.'

'I don't think the curorium is open,' said Seth.

'No matter, I'll pop in the back way. They won't mind me.' He slammed the door on his way out, causing all the charms and chimes to clamour angrily.

At that moment, their chiming sounded to Seth like mocking laughter.

The back way into the curorium. Of course there was a back way! How could he have failed to register the significance of that narrow passage directly from the street into the walled courtyard? He really had failed as a detective, because that meant pretty much anyone could have slipped in there to steal Tendril Vetch's jade bottle.

The door chimes tinkled again.

Seth struggled to bring his mind back on to his

work and push aside his dismay that his careful list of prime suspects was utterly worthless. But when he saw who their customer was, he snapped to attention.

29. STRUCK DOWN IN THE COURSE OF HIS DUTY

Kalinder Squerr's high heels clicked as she slowly made her way through the upside-down forest of feathery dreamcatchers. Her critical gaze coolly swept the wall crammed with shelves of different coloured rocks and crystals, with their claims of amazing magical properties.

She was wearing a beautifully cut slate-grey suit and her hair was piled up, twisting that long red stripe elaborately on top of her head. Somehow, even all the dangling dreamcatchers stayed out of her way.

'Mrs Squerr, how can we help?' asked Seth, his squeaky voice betraying his nervousness at the unexpected arrival of the head of MagiCon in their shop.

Cheery rushed out back to drag in Miss Young, who fussed in, smoothed her hair and shrugged off her long coat and stethoscope.

'What an honour,' she said, a little pink in the face. She looked as if she would have rolled out a red carpet if she could.

'Everything well, I trust?' Mrs Squerr enquired in her cool, even voice.

'It's all lovely, thank you so much for coming to my little shop to ask,' replied Miss Young.

What had brought Mrs Squerr from her cool, calm office into this shop full of fake amulets, charms and those awful wiggle worms? Seth felt he was probably in trouble, but wasn't exactly sure which of his recent mistakes had been found out. His heart pounded in fear at the sudden thought that she was here to summon him right now to take his Prospect. He would fail. He had no magic to demonstrate, nothing to offer.

'I have heard such impressive things about this new business, Forever.' Mrs Squerr walked right up to the counter. Her eyes lingered on the weirdly elaborate and difficult-to-read clock. 'I wanted to see it for myself. And to have the chance to thank you for taking on Master Seppi. It is a very great personal favour to me. I do hope he is being useful.' She turned and Seth felt the scrutiny of her intelligent eyes.

'Oh, thank you for sending us Seth.' Miss Young bowed her shining head and only stopped short of bobbing a curtsey. 'Such a thoughtful and genius idea. We have been so busy it has saved me leaving poor Cheery alone. He may be named for the Egyptian god of chaos, but he's been nothing but a steady hand.'

Cheery snorted derisively, pretending it was a cough when she saw Miss Young's sharp glance.

Seth felt hot under their critical gaze.

Miss Young reached anxiously for her tube of Delicious Demise, squirting a dab on the back of one hand. 'I have been so blessed with success with my little shop. And congratulations to you on your promotion,' she gushed.

'I should like to buy one of your famous remedies.' Mrs Squerr's cool appraisal shifted to the towering piles of identical white boxes. 'What do you recommend? I have been hearing very good things about your Perfectly Prime Powders.'

'Oh, you already have the most beautiful skin!' declared Miss Young, peering at Mrs Squerr's hands as if she would like to seize one in hers.

Seth reached for a white box from one of the shelves, but Miss Young was quicker and reached under the counter for a packet and slid that across first.

As Cheery began to ring the price up on the till Miss Young put a hand across her mouth and gave a little giggle. 'I'm sure Mrs Squerr can have the special price,' she whispered and rang in half the usual amount. 'Is there anything else at all we can help with?' she asked, clasping her hands together and looking earnestly at their regal visitor.

'I very much hope there might be. I am assured you can advise me of some sort of lotion that deals with magical curses –' Seth pricked up his ears and Cheery moved in a little closer – 'of the skin.'

Miss Young tried to cover up her surprise. 'I'd need details. I probably need to see the – er – patient.' She stammered slightly. 'Who has been struck? Not you, Mrs Squerr?'

Mrs Squerr allowed an annoyed frown to descend, just for a second, and shook the question away in a gesture that reminded Seth so much of Angelique. 'My young apprentice—' she began.

Cheery couldn't help herself: 'Dagger's been attacked with a curse? *Dagger?*'

'That's terrible. Nothing too distressing, I hope,' twittered Miss Young.

'Dagger's not –' Cheery began to ask, pausing as Mrs Squerr's gaze locked on to hers. 'He's not . . . asleep?'

'He has been struck down in the course of his duty. With an unsightly charm.'

Seth and Cheery exchanged a glance. This was the first they'd heard of Dagger being cursed. Even Armory Opal hadn't mentioned it. When had it happened?

Miss Young fluttered: 'Oh, for a moment there we thought . . .' She squidged another blob of Delicious Demise on to her hands and rubbed it in well, releasing a waft of rosewater. 'Of the skin, did you say? I'd be more than happy to make a special preparation. Would he like a home visit? These things can be so unsightly.'

'Is it another of these apprentice attacks?' asked Cheery, her curiosity overcoming any shyness about questioning Mrs Squerr. 'When did it happen? How did it happen? Is that why we haven't seen him today?'

'We are still referring to them as pranks,' was Mrs Squerr's only response to Cheery's rapid-fire questions, a delicate furrow appearing between her eyes.

'Such a brave boy,' sighed Miss Young. 'What are the symptoms? Do you know exactly what terrible spell has been cast on that poor boy? It would help.'

'We are pretty sure of the curse. It's a quite colour-less liquid potion, and although it smells a little antiseptic, it is completely tasteless in food and drink, so not difficult to slip in without someone's knowledge. But it is banned and sinister magic. MagiCon will be putting full power behind getting to the bottom of who cast this. And making sure they are swiftly and suitably punished.'

Seth had grown hotter as she'd described the spell. But he felt faint as her next words left no room for doubt.

'It gives the skin the appearance of having been attacked by insect bites. The curse is commonly referred to as "fleekies".'

Fleekies.

There was a whooshing noise in Seth's ears and he knew in that horrifying moment that all his worse fears were realized. Tendril Vetch had deceived him and tricked him into making a sinister spell – one that had been cast on Dagger Tourmaline.

MagiCon was investigating and were going to find out everything.

PART FOUR

30. AN ATTACK OF THE FLEEKIES

Miss Young had promised her help in finding a cure for the fleekies spell, but then had rushed away, panicked by how behind she was in her home visits to patients. Cheery offered to mind the shop, reminding Seth that he'd promised to try to work out what plants Calamus had been collecting in the graveyard, and what they might be used for. But that seemed less important than what he now knew, and he didn't move.

Seth expected someone to beat down the door

and drag him away at any moment. His magical career was already over, before it had even begun.

Tendril had cursed Dagger. And Seth had made the dark spell that had done it. Seth felt hollowed out just thinking about the full horror of it.

That sick and woozy feeling he'd had really was because he had done proper magic. But it was a spell that should never be conjured and he was responsible for Dagger being cursed.

Now Seth could see it all. He understood what Tendril had meant when he'd told Seth he had an affinity with curology. Seth had looked at the sooty, impressive result of Tendril's spell against his own, clear and not at all potent-looking, and had thought he'd got it all wrong.

But Seth hadn't got it wrong at all – Ten's spell had been wrong. Tendril had spotted his affinity and used him quite deliberately.

He hadn't meant to make a bad spell, but he had made a lot of stupid decisions and bad judgments. Dagger had been on to Tendril's sinister tendencies from the start and was a much better detective than Seth. That hurt. And Seth had made no secret of the fact that he was Tendril's friend. This was a disaster.

Cheery's voice interrupted his increasingly desperate thoughts.

'No wonder Mrs Squerr was monumentally hacked off. Everyone's already going about saying MagiCon can't protect the apprentices – now their own is cursed. It's bad. It's as bad as it can be.' She started to chew at her fingernails.

'At least it isn't the same attack as on Leaf and Myrtle,' Seth managed to say. It was as much as he could muster. He was certain the minute he was found out, he was going to be chucked out of Gramichee. Forget taking his Prospect. What happened if you were caught conjuring sinister spells?

'Aren't you going to the Elysee library?' Cheery asked. 'Thought you'd like time off. Spend your day wallowing in a load of books on plants and herbs, a young wannabe curologist like you. You'll be like Calamus in no time.'

She had no idea how her words stung him. 'I can't go to the library, can I, Cheery? I haven't passed my Prospect. It's why I got shoved in here for a month.' The words came out much harsher than he'd meant. He felt completely caught, but it was in a trap of his own making.

Cheery took a step backwards in surprise. 'What the hairy fishcakes has got into you? All right. My bad. I'd forgotten you can't get access to the library yet. But it won't be long, not with an affinity with curology. It's a rare skill. Don't think I don't know you've been sneaking next door and taking lessons from Ten.'

She smiled, but her words were knives in his heart. How long would it take her to guess Ten had cursed Dagger and Seth had made the spell?

The awful question that loomed even larger was: what if Dagger had been right from the start, and Ten was responsible for all of the apprentice attacks? Had Seth helped the Apprentice Assassin? How could he have been so stupid and not spotted that he was being tricked? Cheery had joked that the seriousness of the attacks had gone up a gear about the time Seth had arrived in Gramichee. Would everyone think his magic was responsible for all the curses? That *he* was the Apprentice Assassin?

All he could hope was that people would see he wasn't a bad person . . . then he found himself replaying that awful overheard conversation between Angelique and her mother.

'Have you actually asked yourself if teaching him magic is even a good idea? What if he does real harm? You can't afford to feel responsible.'

Even Nightshade had spotted the dangers and warned him he was learning from a dubious apprentice. Why hadn't he listened? Why had he just willingly gone off and done spells with Tendril Vetch?

Could it really be because he had secretly been drawn to Tendril's dark power?

Seth felt quite unable to move. Part of him wanted to go to Inspector Pewter and confess everything, yet he shrank from taking a step that would seal his own fate. He couldn't take the risk that Pewter would have little choice but to arrest him on the spot. What with his *notorious mother*.

What should he do? Confessing would achieve nothing – they already knew it was a fleekies spell that had struck Dagger.

Cheery was beginning to look at him strangely. He mumbled something about being seriously worried that, with Dagger being cursed, the apprentice scheme really was finished.

'But it can't be finished!' Cheery's face looked stricken now too. 'It took a load of convincing my parents to let me come here in the first place. I don't wanna go back and tell 'em they were right. They're not very magical. Don't really get it. They'll tell me it's easier being normal and bundle me off where I've no chance of learning magic.'

Seth forced his own troubles to one side to sound optimistic. 'Don't worry, Cheery.'

But the mention of a school reminded him there was only one person he felt he could tell everything to. Someone who might just see a way out of this horrible mess.

But he hesitated over even that. She would be tainted by her association with a disaster like him. Should he even involve her?

He couldn't. And he'd resolved not to. Angelique was on her own case and it was important she prove herself to her mother. Calling her was only going to confirm everything her mother had said about him. But, then again, she had a right to know . . . He smoothed the wave glass.

Perhaps he should talk to Tendril first.

He slipped out the back, past Nightshade, snoring after another heavy night chasing the mice. She'd be joyful if Seth told her they were returning to the Last Chance Hotel. A voice whispered that she might even be pleased if he told her he was never doing magic again. He stepped into the garden, where the fresh air and the smell of sap made him long to be home and away from all of this.

As he approached the rear door of the curorium, he heard voices and paused. He needed to talk to Ten alone. As he dithered, another voice drifted down to him.

'That was a good trick you played on me!'

Seth swung around, then squinted upwards into the sun to where Granny Onabutter was leaning over her iron balcony.

'Er, trick? What do you mean, trick?'

Had she seen him and Vetch make that fleekies spell? Was it over already?

Granny Onabutter let out one of her blood-curdlingly loud laughs, coughed and went back inside, reappearing with a glass of water.

'Nearly had the fright of my life last night. Couldn't sleep. Came out on to the balcony and there was this *glowing*. Nearly fell over the railing.'

Glowing? He could just about make out that she was pointing at the plants he'd helped Ten re-plant high up on her balcony. That's what had been glowing? The naja berries? Then he was recalling the sly look that had crept over Tendril's face when he'd talked about why he was growing them. He'd said it was because the berries might fetch a lot of money, as they were in short supply. But he made the connection now that naja berries had been on that list Calamus had taken from Seth, saying it was ingredients they would never use – the dubious list Cheery insisted hadn't come from her.

'I'm sorry about that, Granny,' he called up. 'I

didn't mean to give you a fright. To be honest, I didn't know they'd glow and scare you or I'd have warned you.'

So naja berries were the plants that glowed. But what did they do?

It now seemed very important to find out. Because Granny would gossip to everyone that he was trying to grow naja berries. Everything he had done since arriving in Gramichee looked as if it had the stain of dark magic upon it.

'Oh, s'all right. You young people must have a little fun,' said Granny.

Seth's slim hope of redeeming himself might lie in discovering the exact curse behind the Deathly Slumber, because it might not be too late to save Leaf Falling. And all Seth's instincts were telling him the naja berries were important. His instincts were also telling him he was out of time. He had to find a way not to be blamed for everything.

He really had no choice but to involve Angelique. He should confess everything to her before she heard it all from someone else, and hope all his mistakes meant he hadn't ruined her reputation too.

She had also come to his rescue so many times, he was clinging to the faint hope that she might have some idea that could save him.

31. IF THE MOMENT EVER COMES

'Angelique,' Seth whispered nervously into the wave glass in the farthest and darkest corner of the courtyard garden. 'Angelique,' he repeated, less quietly. He had no idea how to use the magical device. 'Angelique!' he tried. Loudly.

'Ssh! Seth, what are you thinking?' hissed a familiar annoyed voice.

The centre of the glass glowed and Angelique's face gradually came into view. Eventually it was strong enough to see the clear lines of expressions on her face. And she looked furious. 'Can you please not shout, I'm in a lunchtime detention.'

Despite all the terrible things happening his side of the wave glass, Seth suddenly had to stifle a snigger.

Angelique heard him. 'Luckily the teacher has fallen asleep,' she snapped. 'Although with your shouting I'm surprised she hasn't woken. I hope this is an emergency.'

'Er, well, you said if there ever was a moment . . . but I guess it's more of a—'

She made a very Angelique noise that sounded like *hrrrrrrrump*.

The first time they had spoken using the wave glass, she'd appeared almost as if she was in the room with him and he'd stepped through easily. But this time she seemed to be hanging back and sitting in a fog.

'Sorry it's a bad time. You want to call me at a better one?'

Angelique huffed again. 'Things are going badly here anyway. Just don't talk so loud. Think I'm going to have to tell my mum I've failed. If I don't get expelled first.'

'You sound miserable.'

'Yes, well, I found another trophy today.'

Seth was about to ask if it was another with his mother's name on.

'A whole row of shiny tennis trophies,' sighed Angelique glumly. 'Kalinder Scarlett Heliotrope Linden engraved over and over. She's so brilliant at everything. I've never won a trophy in my life.'

'I'd forgotten you said your mother was at Stoney Warren too. She was in the shop today.'

'In the shop?' Angelique's tone was instantly nervous. 'To buy something? Word of warning, Seth, don't entirely trust my mother. She usually has her own agenda. She's never completely straight with anyone. She's just a little bit secretive – and if ever she decides to tell me anything, I rarely understand it anyway.'

'Hmm, that reminds me of someone.'

'It does?'

'Angelique, don't you think that is just completely like you?'

'I'm nothing whatsoever like my mother. Anyway, I really hope I'm not risking waking this teacher just to discuss my mother's shopping habits.'

'Actually,' said Seth, not knowing how to begin this conversation, 'I was hoping you might help me track down what some ingredients might be used for.'

'Ingredients? But aren't you apprenticed to someone who makes some sort of magical preparations? Can't you ask her?'

'It's not that easy.'

'Seth – what aren't you telling me? There's something going on, isn't there? You're in trouble.'

'Just a little. Is it that obvious?'

'Seth, you're always in trouble.'

He'd got this far and he knew he had to tell her everything. 'Did I say there have been a couple of pranks played on apprentices?' He knew he had deliberately not mentioned this before.

'Pranks? Where is this emergency?'

'It's complicated.' Seth took a deep breath and rushed on.

She didn't even interrupt to scold him for not telling her any of it before. He recounted the whole terrible story about the pranks and the fleekies and his successful conjuring of a sinister spell that had then been used to curse someone.

'Hmm. It's not good, is it, Seth?' He fully expected her to tell him their friendship was over, but Angelique went on, 'You seem really keen to blame yourself for everything. But what have you really done? You might have conjured that spell, but you didn't cast it. And I'm not as convinced as you that it all means your new friend is responsible for every attack.'

A small bit of hope wanted to slide itself into Seth's terrible feelings. 'But he turned Herb Camphor blue. I think he probably strengthened the charm on the curorium windows. He tricked me into making a sinister potion. And he's Dagger's best suspect.'

'I understand all of that. But wasn't it this girl, Leaf, who put the bunny ears on Tendril? It's not all him. And it sounds like Dagger wouldn't leave him alone, that he was really putting the pressure on. Tendril might have wanted to send a message to back off. OK, the fleekies is a bit extreme. And, final thought – you say he tricked you into making that spell, that he had to because his own magic wasn't good enough? So how did he manage to do good enough magic to attack Myrtle and Leaf?'

Relief washed through Seth as he clung on to this tiny sliver of hope. Angelique was right. If Ten had had to trick Seth into making a powerful spell, it made no sense to think he could have conjured the Deathly Slumber curse.

'You don't think Tendril is the Apprentice Assassin?' He felt he might float all the way up to Granny Onabutter's balcony.

'I can't see how he could be. Although I do think if you are going to practise magic, you might think things through a little more.'

Thinking of Granny's balcony made something else fall into place: naja berries. Now all his thoughts were no longer on his fear he'd helped the Apprentice Assassin, Seth was finally able to get back to why he'd convinced himself to bother Angelique in the first place.

'What do naja berries do?'

'Is this a random question or is there a point?'

Seth explained how he and Cheery had watched the strange glowing plants being picked in the graveyard, about Granny Onabutter's glowing balcony and the dubious list of ingredients.

'That list was weird and full of banned ingredients, but Cheery says she doesn't know where it came from. No one knows what was in that curse put on Myrtle and Leaf. If I could find out that spell, everyone might not think quite so badly of me!' he finished excitedly. This wasn't just important, he had a feeling that the list and those naja berries were key to understanding everything. There had to be a link.

Seth had a good memory for ingredients and listed everything. 'Naja berries are in short supply so what are they used for?'

'You want me to look up all those ingredients to see if they all might be in the spell? You're far more expert at what herbs and things do. Not sure I'll be much help.'

'You're in a school, there are a lot of clever people about. You might be able to find someone who knows what they all do. Could they be used together in a spell to put people to sleep?' Seth was remembering how carefully Calamus had screwed up that list, and how he'd mentioned something else . . . 'Calamus mentioned the Oakmore Prophecy as well. Might want to look into that. It could be important.'

Angelique answered with another of her annoyed puffs. 'I'll try, but the chemistry teacher is the one who's disappeared. So, did you get anywhere trying to find out anything about my case you said you'd help with? That trace of magic you took away with you?'

'Er . . .'

She gave a trademark weary sigh. 'You ask for my help. Yet you have completely failed in your promise to help me.'

'Sorry, Angelique.' Seth had completely forgotten, just like he'd forgotten to open the cellar door for Nightshade.

He reached into one of his many pockets guiltily and lifted out the small jar containing the blackened, dried substance he'd scraped from where it had dripped and solidified on the underside of the school desk.

'It's proving tricky,' he said evasively. He was always promising not to let Angelique down, but somehow he always did. He lifted the lid and took an exploratory sniff. The smell was unusual, and it did remind him of something. 'How's your case?'

Angelique's sigh turned into a full-on groan. 'Even Elfreda Oldcastle's records are missing. She cleared out everything. Not so much as a photograph for me to go on. I can't be a complete and utter failure on the first assignment my mother has sent me on. I'm relying on you and that chunk of gunk, Seth. Just use your nose. It's the only sign that there is something magical behind her disappearance. OK, teacher's stirring.'

The connection ended.

Seth felt he now had about a dozen things he needed to do. Would Cheery manage without him? And would he ever manage without Angelique?

32. Naja Berries and Glychwychyn

Taking a moment in his store-cupboard bedroom, Seth slumped on one of the vats of sticky cream and ran his hands through his untidy hair. Nightshade was sleeping, curled up next to one of the warm pipes.

'If I could help MagiCon with their case . . . maybe people would forgive me for being tricked into using bad magic. Where did that list of unusual ingredients come from, Nightshade?' he muttered. 'Is it for a spell? And what does it do?'

'Pigeons!' cried Nightshade in her sleep.

He could remember the list, but he wrote it out anyway, hoping the process might give him a fresh idea. Naja berries, glychwychyn, belladonna, acacia bark, alpaca calfsfoot jelly, trefoil root. 'Belladona I've heard of,' murmured Seth. 'In ancient times it was used in beauty products. Dad taught me all sorts like that. I know it's a dark berry. Sometimes it's called deadly nightshade. Have I told you that you are named after a poison?'

Could it be the spell that had been used in the attacks?

He should just go around to the curorium and demand answers. Or, more appealingly, he could try to find a time when it was empty, sneak in and look it up himself in Calamus's books.

Nightshade stirred. 'Have you got that cellar door open yet?' she asked, taking him completely by surprise. He hadn't thought she'd been listening.

Seth instantly felt guilty again. As well as forgetting Angelique had asked for his help, this was something else he had failed to do. She was right about the door being locked. He had tried it, but hadn't come up with any good reason to ask for the key. He got to his feet and let Nightshade fall back to sleep. She was exhausted. She'd told him she wanted to go home. But right now he needed answers. He had to stop letting people down.

He stole out of the back door and into the tall, thick greenery of the courtyard garden. The back door to the curorium was slightly ajar. He slipped through, pushing aside the long dragon curtain. The smell of bonfires was strong, and there was something else in the air, something pungent, something familiar. Wild garlic? Limeflower? Most importantly, no Calamus at his desk. Seth seized his chance and crept into the unlit front of the shop. He wanted to scour the bookshelves and see if he could find a mention of any of those ingredients.

As he swept towards the books, a sound startled him into questioning whether he was really alone. He turned. A movement in a corner, low to the ground. The darkness had covered the fact that there was a figure in dark clothes crouching, almost invisibly.

Seth stopped moving, all his senses alert.

There was a low groan and the crouching figure turned. Seth had been expecting Tendril Vetch to be the one looking up at him, but he saw the shocking features of Dagger Tourmaline, his smooth pale skin blemished with ugly red weals.

Seth flinched. This was what his fleekies spell had

done to the handsome young apprentice.

'I can't believe it . . . I just found him,' groaned Dagger, still crouched on the floor.

Seth took a step closer, and that's when he realized he had caught Dagger leaning over someone lying completely still on the floor.

'He was like this when I got here.'

It took a moment before Seth could make out the bat-like grey hair and the gold-striped waistcoat. 'Mr Opal! Is he all right?'

'All right? He's dead!'

33. The End of the Apprenticeships

Seth felt for a pulse, any sort of life signs, to prove Tourmaline wrong. He had to be wrong. Armory Opal could not be dead. He'd be like Leaf. In a really deep sleep.

But there was no hopeful pulse.

From behind the dragon curtain came a sneeze.

The twitching of the curtain seemed to bring Tourmaline out of his shocked state. He rose from his crouched position and rushed, grabbing at the figure lurking there and dragging it through. It was

Tendril Vetch. Dagger twisted Ten's arm up behind his back so that the boy cried out.

'Vetch! You have really done it this time. You've killed the Apprentice Finder and you tried to pin it on me!'

Tendril's eyes widened with fright and disbelief and he began to babble. 'But I was out. I didn't know he was coming and I didn't know you would even be here. It's all a mistake.' He looked imploringly at Seth. 'Seth – you have to believe me, I—'

'Save it for the judge,' growled Dagger.

Seth could only watch helplessly as Tourmaline dragged the boy away.

'Well, MagiCon have really let everyone down.' Granny Onabutter jabbed to remove Gorgeous Tom and plonked herself into the lips chair. 'Couldn't solve the case of a missing pair of mittens. Not even if they were in their own pockets. And I heard they are covering up that Myrtle Rust died. The apprentice scheme will be scrapped and no mistake!'

Seth just stood by the window, feeling dazed and overwhelmed, wishing they hadn't had to open the Belle Boutique today. He couldn't bear the thought of talking to anyone, even Granny. He couldn't quite believe her curranty eyes shone as if she was at a birthday party. 'The apprentice scheme has twisted into something dark and terrible. The Apprentice Finder himself, a victim!'

Cheery surprised Seth by bursting into tears.

Granny Onabutter had the grace to look ashamed, and hustled herself out, muttering. Seth was glad to see her go. Cheery heaved herself out of her beanbag.

'We won't let it be the end of everything.' Seth busied himself making tea and handed Cheery a mug.

The tinkling of the door announced they had another customer and he forced himself to find a smile, but was relieved to see it was only Miss Young returning exhausted from another home visit. Seth offered her tea. She took it gratefully and leant her forehead against the cool wall behind the counter. They all muttered that they couldn't believe it.

'Granny Onabutter says the apprenticeships will be over,' said Cheery, sounding steadfast and not giving away that she'd had a big wobble only moments ago. 'Are you going to send us home?'

Miss Young rubbed in a little Delicious Demise before sinking into the lips chair. 'They may give me no choice. But I need my apprentices. Let's shut up shop. No one will complain if we close early.'

Cheery hinted Miss Young might treat them to a bun at the Scrum, but Miss Young said all she was good for was a lie-down. Seth steered Cheery out into the cool freshness of the garden, where it felt like the promise of spring had been shoved aside by low, threatening cloud and the cold bite of approaching rain. An early dark was creeping in. Nightshade slipped out too and started to wash her whiskers.

'I guess that's it – Ten must have killed Opal.' Cheery didn't find a place to sit and sip her tea, but prowled like a tiger. 'But why? Not being able to come up with any good reason is what made me keep telling Dagger he must be on the wrong track.'

'It was Tourmaline I found crouched over a dead body. If I hadn't gone in right that moment he could have slipped out and no one would have known he was there.'

'You think Dagger killed Opal?' Cheery held Seth with a keen look over the rim of her cup. 'I know he has ambitions to make a name for himself, but killing two people? And I thought you were more fixated on it being Calamus and that still has to be more likely. Oh, and wasn't Armory Opal one of your top suspects? I'm thinking him being dead puts him out of the running.'

'Could it be a terrible accident?' suggested Seth.

'Oops, I just killed two sorcerers? That's some accident. No way. Whatever spell killed them would take skill to put together. It is just possible Tendril learnt enough from Calamus. But I still reckon on it being Calamus himself.'

Inspector Pewter and Calamus might not get along, but Pewter trusted the curologist. Unless the inspector was wrong? And Seth had talked it all through with Angelique, and they'd agreed pinning everything on Tendril was a little too convenient.

'I still think Dagger is suspicious,' he said carefully. 'Right from the start he was determined to convince everyone it's all down to Ten. He was relentless, even when Calamus gave him an alibi which should have made him look elsewhere. You've spent ages in the Scrum with Dagger. What do you really think?'

Cheery looked thoughtful. 'Tendril wanted to prank Leaf to get her back for the bunny ears. Leaf was attacked and they found the jade bottle. Maybe you're right and it's just too convenient.'

'Myrtle was the first victim. Was Myrtle involved in the pranks? Did she play one on Ten?'

'Do you know, I don't think Myrtle was involved in the pranks at all. Calamus is the one with the skills. And we caught him picking those dodgy plants,' insisted Cheery.

'And Nightshade worked out that Calamus saying he was with Ten was a clever way of giving himself an alibi,' said Seth slowly.

'Your cat said that?'

'Erm, well, sometimes I kind of imagine what she might say. But you are right. It all comes back to the spell that was used,' said Seth, happy to dodge any questions about Nightshade. He might not want to reveal he had a talking cat, but he decided it was time to trust Cheery a little bit more. 'The thing is, I actually have a friend looking into those ingredients from the list . . .'

It had grown completely dark by the time he'd finished telling Cheery about Angelique. He'd held back as much as he could about her undercover investigation – that wasn't his secret to share. The garden was now lit by only a fragile bit of moonlight high above and even that was mostly obscured by clouds. 'Let's hope Angelique has found naja berries put you into a deep, deep sleep,' Seth finished.

'Talking about graveyards and weird plants, did you brush against them when we were having our party with the bones of the dead?' Cheery pointed to Seth's stomach.

Something luminous had somehow attached itself to him. He fumbled to find out what was giving off that tiny glow. From a pocket he pulled out a glass jar – the one in which he'd collected that cinder globule in the abandoned chemistry lab of Stoney Warren School for Superior Girls. This hardened blob was Angelique's clue – the only indication that there was anything magical about Elfreda Oldcastle's disappearance. Now it was glowing. As did the plants in the graveyard and up on Granny's balcony.

'That glow is just like those plants we saw Calamus collecting,' said Cheery, voicing his thoughts. 'Sort of pink and luminous. So where d'you get that? Whatever is it?'

Seth stared at the jar, groping to make the connection that must be there. 'I think it's the moonlight that's making them glow. Don't give up on your apprenticeship yet, Cheery. I think I know why this case has been so difficult to fathom. I think it's because part of the answer doesn't lie in Gramichee at all – some of the answers lie in Stoney Warren School for Superior Girls. Don't ask me yet, but I think we should talk to Angelique right now.'

'And how are we going to do that?'

Seth took out the wave glass.

34. Deeply Magical Properties

'Are you doing magic, Seth?' Cheery watched him brush his fingers across the wave glass. 'Wow, let's see!'

'Not my magic. My friend set it all up.'

Angelique's voice came through quickly and crisply. 'What is it with you? Can't you understand that a wave glass isn't just for every time you feel lonely and fancy a chat?'

Seth grinned sheepishly at Cheery. 'She's always pleased to hear from me, honest. Angelique, it's another emergency.'

'I've never known anyone have quite as many emergencies as you, Seth Seppi.'

Seth quickly updated her about Armory Opal's death and how everyone was predicting the end of the apprentice scheme and he and Cheery were determined to solve the case and make sure that didn't happen. But how they were short on any sort of proof. He finished, waiting with great anticipation for news on those ingredients.

'All right, that's bad,' Angelique whispered. 'But I don't think you'll like what I've found. I'm afraid I think you're on the wrong track. I'm in the library now. Your naja berries are really interesting. Did you know they have five tastes? Sweet, salty, bitter, umami and sour – all at the same time. And they are rare.'

'Are they used in sinister magic?'

'Well, they wouldn't be used for putting anyone to sleep. They are rumoured to have restorative properties connected to longevity.'

Cheery blinked twice. 'Say that in English,' she said into the glass.

'The folklore is that they have rejuvenating properties, that they help you to have a long life. Kind of the opposite of putting you to sleep, really – but that's if they actually do anything at all. They're rarely used in regular magic. Sorry.'

'Is that her idea of explaining things?' said Cheery, peering over Seth's shoulder.

'I mean I only found them in books about the sort of witchy nonsense and fantasy magic that belongs in stories,' Angelique explained. She forgot to whisper and finished with a loud tut.

'You mean the magic that regular people think sorcerers do?' put in Cheery. 'Like finding treasure at the end of a rainbow, being able to turn any metal into gold, reversing the ageing process or finding those genies in bottles that grant you three wishes?'

'That's exactly what I mean,' said Angelique. 'It's the same thing with your Oakmore Prophecy, which I also looked into – see how hard I'm working on *your* problem. It's another of those impossible bits of magic. The sort that non-magical people like to get excited about.'

'So, why have naja berries suddenly gone into short supply?' floundered Seth. 'I was really hoping they'd be in the Deathly Slumber curse.'

'I've scribbled you a few notes about what I've found,' said Angelique. 'The headlines are, neither naja berries nor the Oakmore Prophecy are anything to do with putting people to sleep. Sorry, Seth.'

Seth thanked her. He was going to have to think everything through all over again. He'd had such a strong feeling they'd been on the right track. He was missing something. Being so wrong about the naja berries almost made him not mention the rest, but Cheery gave him a painful nudge and pointed to the glowing cinder.

'OK, here's the other thing. I think our two cases might be connected. Three words – glowing pink substances.'

'Is that *your* idea of explaining things?' Angelique sighed.

'It might be easier to show you. Can you come through?' suggested Seth.

Even through the narrow aperture of the wave glass, Seth could see Angelique's shoulders slump. 'But if I leave it'll mean I've failed! I never thought I'd fail!'

'Angelique, you are not going to fail. You never fail at anything. Maybe we can work together. I had a hunch that naja berries might be linked to your teacher disappearing, but I've gone wrong somewhere.'

'How is that even possible? Naja berries aren't even commonly used in magic.'

He'd been so sure Calamus had been picking naja

berries in the graveyard. Naja berries had been on that list. They glowed. And the substance that Angelique had found at the school had the same pinkish glow about it. But the link that seemed so right was wrong somehow. It was as if he was looking at everything all twisted, a bit like Nightshade had said about Gramichee. *This whole place is trying too hard to not appear what it really is.*

'I don't know. Maybe some of the pupils were secretly doing this kind of fantasy magic. And the missing teacher found them and stopped them.'

'What – you think the pupils done her in?' suggested Cheery.

'It makes no less sense than anything else I've come up with,' groaned Angelique. 'But I have to say the most exciting thing I've found the students doing is inventing a sleeping championship. They actually awarded a trophy to someone who broke the record and did not move out of bed for seven days. Oh, this case is impossible!' she cried. 'I've started to think sending me here was my mother just . . .'

She tailed off, but Seth felt pretty sure he could guess what she'd almost said. She was suspicious that she'd been despatched on this unimportant case purely so Mrs Squerr could separate her utterly brilliant daughter from the dead weight of helping someone as unreliable and untalented at magic as he was. Angelique was humiliated by not being able to solve it.

'Two people have *died* here, Angelique. Please.'

'Fine! But I am definitely changing out of this school uniform.'

Angelique looked much more her usual self when she stepped into the garden. She was dressed in the black suit that fitted her so well she could be both smart and deadly effective. She was also gripping her red divinoscope and Seth realized how very much it was part of her. She stood there, dappled by moonbeams. And she looked ready for anything.

Cheery's eyes widened when she spied the silver-topped cane. 'That's some sort of magical instrument, isn't it?' She reached for it eagerly.

Seth saw Angelique hesitate. He knew how precious it was to her. It was also just sinking in that he'd revealed Angelique's undercover mission to Cheery without asking for permission. He just hoped he hadn't blown it at the school itself by using the wave glass.

'Magic leaves ripples in the air,' Angelique explained, reluctantly letting Cheery examine the divinoscope. She told her the sort of things it helped

267

her detect, like how long ago magic was used and even the types of magic. 'Sometimes I can even unpick exactly what spell was cast. But that takes years of practice. I'm only a beginner really.'

'Yeah, well,' Cheery stroked the cane adoringly, 'I've got an idea. You can tell if anything Miss Young produces has any actual magic in it. Then I can find out once and for all if I'm totally wasting my time with this apprenticeship. Then I might not be so upset if the whole thing collapses.'

'I hardly need a sensitive magical instrument to give you the answer about those overpriced amulets she's flogging.' Angelique sniffed.

'You told Mr Opal you think Miss Young is a fraud, didn't you?' Seth asked Cheery.

She stuck out her chin. 'I may have dropped a hint or two. Well, it's my time she's wasting.'

'Talking of wasting time,' said Angelique, getting down to business, 'you were going to explain how a dried blob in an abandoned school chemistry lab and a teacher vanishing could possibly be linked to a lot of people in Gramichee being attacked. And why all that means I had to give up on my case before it was solved.'

'Of course.' Seth didn't like to admit that he already felt so much better just having her there, or that it was a bit like trying to juggle too many mis-matched things with one hand. Or that he had absolutely no plan at all for what to do next. He was going to have to think hurriedly; he needed to start working out how it was all connected.

But a plan was just starting to form. He did have an idea of what he needed to do next. 'Didn't you say Stoney Warren once belonged to a magical family but their magic died out?'

Angelique nodded.

'And naja berries are not sinister magic – right?'

She gave another nod.

'Right, erm, well, actually, in that case, I need to pop out.'

'You've dragged me off my case urgently and now you've decided to go out?'

'I won't be long, honestly.'

'I'll just hang around and wait for you, shall I?'

'That would be great! Cheery, could you possibly fill in anything Angelique wants to know? And Angelique, you could poke around with the divinoscope – maybe you can see if Cheery's suspicions about Miss Young's magic are right!'

'I do not *poke around* with my divinoscope,' sniffed Angelique.

Cheery fixed Seth with a familiar you-are-toast

look. 'Tell me what you are up to?'

Seth's face lost its smile. Having Angelique here made him brave enough to do something he probably should have done a while back. He cleared his throat. 'I'm going to do what I should have done days ago. I'm going to face Calamus.'

35. CONFESSION

Seth was surprised to find that, for the first time, the front door of the curorium moved fluidly at his touch. It was as if he was expected. He pushed it slowly, inhaling the overwhelming smell of smouldering bonfires as he stepped into the gloomy shop.

He tried to ignore how loudly his heart was beating. He hoped Angelique was right and that those naja berries were not some sort of sinister ingredient. If she was, there should be no problem with him asking Calamus about them . . . no problem at all.

The white-haired old man was hunched at his workbench, poring over the cracked pages of one of his ancient books, and didn't even look up as a breeze drifted past, lifting the heavy dragon curtain and announcing Seth's arrival more subtly than the frenzied tinkling of chimes and charms at Miss Young's.

'If you are looking for an apprenticeship, don't bother – I wish to retire,' came Calamus's cracked voice. 'This brave new scheme, so wondrously inclusive of all with a spark of magic, no matter what their background. Always predicted it'd be trouble.'

Seth's mouth felt too dry to swallow as he stepped further into the room. If there was one person in Gramichee he really did not trust, it was this old man, weaving spells with his yellow fingers.

Even so, Seth responded staunchly. 'Some say it's brave, and the only way to save the magical world. Magic is dying out. You and the other principals have got so much to offer. Anyway, Ten will be back – when all of this is sorted out.'

Calamus hunched further forward, his white straggly hair shielding his scarred face like a curtain. 'You think I should have been quicker to spot what was happening? You think I should have known my apprentice has been causing trouble? You are right!

I won't be taking any more. I'm too old. Look elsewhere.'

Seth moved to stand right alongside him. 'I didn't come here to ask for his apprenticeship. I don't believe Ten is responsible – at least not for everything. I came to ask for your help. If we can work out what curse was used on Leaf Falling we might still save her. And you . . . you recognized ingredients on a list I had. Sinister ingredients, you said.'

'And Armory Opal?' said Calamus. 'Myrtle? Nothing's going to bring them back.'

'Well, no, but—'

'He was my apprentice,' Calamus went on. His voice was quiet, but there was no mistaking the anger. 'And what did he do? Used my ingredients, my grimoires, abused my trust and my teaching and twisted it for his own personal vendettas. You think I should let him back? I can't work with an apprentice so easily lured to the sinister side. It takes courage to resist and without that strength, he shouldn't be learning at all.'

None of this was what Seth had been expecting. He hadn't thought Calamus would speak at such length, so passionately. He was completely wrong-footed to be facing this sad old man.

Once again it looked like Seth had been seeing

things wrongly. He had to remind himself that Calamus was still a strong suspect, even though Inspector Pewter trusted him.

'Do you think Tendril could do the advanced magic that cursed Myrtle, Leaf and Armory Opal?'

Did Calamus really believe it was all down to Tendril? If so, it was doubly confusing that he'd falsely given him an alibi . . . unless Nightshade was right and he was covering his own tracks.

'Why did you say Ten was with you and couldn't have cursed Leaf?' challenged Seth, hardly feeling Calamus would answer.

But he answered readily enough. 'I thought Tourmaline was targeting him. I thought it was my duty to protect him as his principal. I was misguided. He used blue magic on the Camphor boy, but I was fool enough to believe that was the worst of it.' His voice was almost a whisper as he carried on piecing together a spell.

'You know more than anyone about ingredients, their powers and uses. Will you help me find what spell was used?'

Calamus turned, but Seth had prepared himself not to flinch and stare at the pink and puckered side of his face.

'You know I cannot. I hoped I had done enough

for this town. But clearly not enough to make amends. Miss Young, with her pretty face and her winning ways, has found stealing my business all too easy. Winning the trust of people is hard. It doesn't matter how much good I do. But, perhaps I am not being honest . . .' He allowed a small smile to crack his withered lips. 'Perhaps people don't judge me too harshly. Perhaps it's time to admit that the attacks are on my conscience.'

Was this a confession?

Seth felt completely wrong-footed again, and unsure what to do next. But Calamus just went back to drawing bottles towards him, following the instructions from the book on the workbench, as though the conversation was over.

Had Seth just heard him admit to the attacks?

Seth went hot and then cold.

Calamus surprised him by carrying on talking. 'Yes, young Vetch took me by surprise. I failed to see how skilled he had become. I failed . . . and then he went on and made the banned spell that has so disfigured the young MagiCon apprentice. Successfully conjuring that spell for fleekies showed me what he was capable of. My eyes were finally opened. Some might say it is wrong to be impressed that he'd advanced himself that far without me instructing him. It's not the first time I have made mistakes, misjudgements. His magic is amazing. And all I have done is enabled him to use it for unwise things. Perhaps it's not such a bad thing that the apprentice scheme is over.'

Tendril was under arrest, and even his own principal wasn't going to defend him because he believed he'd successfully conjured that fleekies spell.

Only Tendril hadn't done that spell.

'It's not over – not yet,' said Seth quietly. He really had no idea what to do, what to say. 'It's a good scheme. And you are a great principal. In fact, people say you are the best.'

'Such a great principal – allowing my apprentice to practise sinister magic.'

Still Seth hesitated.

'Because Tendril did that fleekies spell, you think he attacked all the apprentices? Up until you found out about that, you hadn't thought his magic was good enough, right? But now you think he's capable, you won't stand by him and won't take him back?'

'Now you understand. I cannot afford to keep making mistakes,' Calamus went on. He pointed to his ruined face. 'I got this in the Unpleasant – no doubt Sagacious Pewter has told you as much. Unlike others who have managed to conceal their involvement in that terrible event, I carry my mistake around with me – a reminder to me and everyone, always.' He turned then, away from Seth and back to his book. 'So I am to retire.'

Seth still didn't move.

'You are still standing there? I can see I am not convincing you. Well, let me also tell you this – I was impressed by that fleekies spell and I shouldn't have been. I could not see beyond that truly remarkable magic. Just don't go repeating that I said so. It does me no good to be impressed by sinister magic. So no more apprentices.'

There was only one way to get Calamus to stop thinking like this.

Seth had to confess to having performed that sinister spell.

He had made that spell – tricked into it by Tendril, but he had been the one who had conjured it.

He didn't want to have to take the enormous step of admitting the truth to Calamus and face the consequences. But what choice did he have?

'It wasn't Tendril who conjured the fleekies spell,' he said, speaking quickly before he could change his mind, almost whispering the words. 'He doesn't have the dark power you are accusing him of. It was me.'

36. YOUR POWER UNLEASHED iNTO THAT SPELL

Calamus didn't look at him after he'd made the confession, but continued sorting through his glass jars.

Seth waited. He'd just confessed to having performed sinister magic and he was already regretting having spoken up so quickly. He'd only meant to come here to plead for Calamus's help in finding answers, seeking knowledge about those ingredients and a cure. Now the horrible truth was out there.

When a question came, the old man's voice didn't

sound so weary, but there was also no accusation in it, only curiosity. 'Who's been training you?'

Seth swallowed down his first answer. How easily the wrong words might spell trouble for Angelique, and he would do anything to prevent making her situation any worse than it already was.

'I've taught myself. I'm not very good. Ten told me I'd done it right, but I didn't believe him. Please believe me when I say I had no idea what spell I was doing.'

All his deepest fears had just been confirmed. Calamus had told him it was really impressive magic that he'd done. But it was of the wrong sort. He had an affinity with strongly sinister spells. He had to give up magic – now.

Calamus moved away abruptly from his work-bench and came close to Seth, bringing that smell of burning, as if he also carried around the very flames that had scarred him. 'You know you got it all wrong?'

Seth gulped, stood his ground, but was puzzled. 'But you just said it was a good, strong spell, I—'

'You put far too much of yourself into it.'

Seth was silent. He had no idea what Calamus was talking about and was afraid he was going to say the wrong thing.

Calamus moved closer and fixed Seth with a penetrating look from his heavily lidded eyes. 'Dragons preserve us. You've got a power, boy. Magic crackles in you like lightning. Do you know how dangerous you could actually be if someone doesn't take you in hand and teach you how to rein it in?'

Seth had no answer. All thoughts of asking about that list seemed far less important than simply getting out of here as quickly as possible before he admitted to anything even worse.

But the old man was going on. 'You don't know what I'm talking about, do you?'

Seth shook his head.

'I knew right away Tendril wasn't responsible for that fleekies spell. It's no surprise to me that it was you.'

Seth's insides ran cold. So Calamus had tricked him into making that confession. What was going to happen now?

'Don't you know what happens with untrained magic? Let me warn you. You blew a whole load of your sorcerer energy into that fleekies spell, and it really didn't need it. You made it even more powerful. Dragons' teeth! That poor Tourmaline boy. With your power unleashed into that spell, I expect that handsome face of his will always bear the scars you gave him. Living life with scars. That's something I understand. You need to know enough to stop yourself!'

'I-I didn't know,' said Seth weakly. This seemed such a pitiful defence. He should have known. He had feared for months now that his power was a dark one. Hadn't he always known that his magic seemed different, much more uncontrollable than everyone else's?

And now questions were coming that he knew he shouldn't even have. Because what Calamus had said about his power gave him a giddy rush of incredible but utterly misplaced joy. And then terrible guilt. He wanted to be thrilled to hear he might one day be a powerful sorcerer – the thought made him dizzy – but was he destined to contaminate every spell he ever tried?

Was that why his magic was so uncontrollable? Because his magic was so strong? Strong, but it belonged to the wrong side, which meant he had to give it up. He had vowed never to use sinister magic.

But how strong am I? How strong could he be if he could find the right person to teach him? *No!* There were too many risks.

Calamus's eyes were focused in the far distance. 'How did you feel after you'd made it?' His voice betrayed only light curiosity, but his pale eyes moved to bore into Seth.

Seth didn't want to be forced to talk about doing sinister magic. He was horrified at the excitement that had briefly coursed through him at the thought of power.

He just wanted to get out of there, but Calamus was waiting for an answer. And there was no point lying. He was going to have to own up if he was to save Tendril from taking the full blame for everything that had happened.

'I felt so weak,' confessed Seth. 'Just another example of why I am never going to make it as a sorcerer. I think I actually blacked out. Tendril gave me something that tasted like hot chocolate. He told me it was expensive and not to tell you he'd given me it.'

Calamus gave a dry chuckle, like leaves rustling. 'You shouldn't put yourself at risk like that. Especially not if you want to study to become a curologist. Or live to become an old curologist like me.'

Seth couldn't help it – now he wanted to know different answers to different questions. 'What happened when I did that spell? What do you mean I put some of myself into it? I don't understand.'

'Some sorcerers are more naturally powerful than

others. Even you, green and tender as a new shoot in Gramichee, must have noticed that? Some struggle their whole lives to do even a basic spell. Partly that is because when you do magic, some of it comes from you. Hasn't someone told you this?' Calamus tutted loudly. 'If you are sizzling with magical force, you must learn to do magic in almost the opposite way to how most people struggle.'

Actually, people probably had been trying to tell him all this, he'd just never properly understood it before. But it was a little too late to get it now.

'You need to be far more careful,' Calamus continued. 'For you, learning magic isn't about straining every sinew, it's about reining yourself in. That's every bit as hard, if not harder, but if you don't, you could do some damage – not least to yourself. And there are those in Gramichee and beyond who would be very happy indeed to recruit you. They'd use you. Your magic. Vetch spotted it. You were too easy to trick into producing a spell that was beyond him. Don't go around letting on about the power you are holding there, boy. Because Vetch won't be the last to try to use it.'

How terrible that I did that to Dagger, Seth thought. *But right now my problems aren't important*. He'd come here because if they failed to find answers the apprentice scheme was over. He had to focus, persuade Calamus to talk to him. Before anyone else died.

'Now you know it wasn't Vetch who did that powerful magic, will you help me?' Seth realized he no longer found the puckered skin on the old man's face disturbing. 'You're the only one who can cure them.'

The curologist shook his head. 'You ask too much. Miss Young has arrived and Gramichee has turned its back on me. It's about time I turned my back on Gramichee. I am going to retire. Besides, that magic is something even I have never seen before. I don't think there is anything anyone can do.'

37. The Apprentice Assassin Strikes Again

At least Seth now understood that drained feeling that had come over him. It was doing magic. But it wasn't because he was no good – it was that he wasn't keeping his magic in check.

Now he understood that, there might have been a chance for his magic to finally get better. But he felt surer than ever that if he did carry on, he wouldn't become the powerful sorcerer of his dreams. He'd turn into the sinister kind of his nightmares.

There are those in Gramichee and beyond who

would be very happy indeed to recruit you. They'd use you. Your magic, Calamus had warned.

Seth was dangerous, and other sorcerers might recruit him to achieve their sinister ends. Hadn't he heard Kalinder Squerr warning her daughter about him? *Have you actually asked yourself if teaching him magic is even a good idea? What if he does real harm?* Mrs Squerr had challenged Angelique, warning her to steer clear of Seth and his strange explosive magic.

She had been right. What would Mrs Squerr say when she learnt Seth had been involved in doing the powerful sinister magic that had struck down the MagiCon apprentice? Angelique had put her faith in the wrong person. Well, he wasn't going to let her take any blame. If only he hadn't called Angelique through the wave glass just now. How he wished he'd gone to Calamus first.

Seth stepped quietly into the kitchen prep area, surprised to find Cheery tidying. She looked at him expectantly for news and he remembered that he'd promised to come back quickly with a plan of what they should do next.

He asked where Angelique was and Cheery told him she was still taking readings with her divinoscope.

'Think she's *still* in your store cupboard, but she's

a bit secretive, isn't she?' finished Cheery.

Seth guessed Angelique hadn't shared anything her readings might be telling her, but then Seth was used to that. He dragged his feet slowly through to his bedroom store cupboard, hoping a plan of what to say would suddenly come to him.

As he walked along the short, dark corridor he noticed something that shouldn't be there. He had to get close before he realized what he was looking at – a slumped shape at the very end of the corridor, right by the door to the cellar. His heart started to hammer, yet time seemed to slow as he inched closer to what he knew was a body, lying flat on the ground. A human shape. Unmoving. Just like Armory Opal.

But this shape was far more familiar. Her glossy hair was spread around her, its dramatic red stripe catching the little light there was. Without even daring to breathe, Seth bent, feeling desperately for a pulse.

Please don't let her be dead, not her.

Her divinoscope was lying next to her, but Seth reached for her hand, flung out towards the hockey stick from the storeroom. Had she used it to fight whoever had attacked her? Few people took Angelique by surprise.

This could not be happening. Angelique was so

smart, so powerful. It was impossible that she should be forever asleep.

Then he felt it. A pulse. Fine and trembling, as if he was holding a bird. But it was there. Whatever it took, Seth would fight to make sure this was not a deathly slumber from which she would never reawaken. She would not die like Myrtle Rust.

She had never given up on him, and he wouldn't give up on her. To lose her was beyond his imagining.

PART FIVE

38. Impossible Spells and Terrible Curses

Seth had barely registered the two magical doctors who came to carry Angelique away to Ward 23. He was aware of little, and what he did feel didn't seem real.

Cheery had eventually found him and sprung into action, calling the doctors straight away before ushering Seth into his bedroom-cupboard with orders to rest. For all Seth knew, he might have been there for hours, gripping Angelique's hand, willing it to all be some terrifying mistake.

When he walked into the shop the next morning, Cheery handed him a mug of tea along with a scrap of paper. 'The notes Angelique made for you. She gave them to me, before . . . They'll find a cure, try not to worry.'

Seth stuffed the notes into one of his tunic pockets. Could Angelique be cured? Even Calamus had said it was magic like he'd never seen and he feared nothing could be done. He sipped the tea, his whole body trembling as slumped into Cheery's beanbag.

Nightshade leapt on to his lap and lay down. Her warmth was like a comforting hot water bottle, but Seth didn't need comforting. He needed something to sharpen his senses, something to wake him properly so he could think and act.

He got a long sharp claw in the leg.

The clamour of chimes announced a customer.

'You'd think Miss Young would close and put her money-making on hold for one day,' Cheery groaned, shooing Seth out back.

For one terrible moment, Seth imagined it was going to be Mrs Squerr, blaming him for what had happened, but no doubt she was maintaining a bedside vigil in Ward 23. He practically ran to his cupboard just in case, and crawled cowardly into his hammock.

He felt the full force not only of his failure, but also guilt. He'd broken his resolve not to bother Angelique, to sort out things on his own, and now she was at death's door. It was all his fault.

'So, who's smacked her with a curse?' asked Nightshade as she eased herself into the unsteady hammock in the overheated store cupboard. She crawled on to his stomach and began to prick him with needle-sharp claws. 'Thought you were close to an answer?'

'Every time I try to do something I make things worse.'

'I don't think you can actually make things worse this time. Angelique's been hit by powerful sinister magic. You've always had doubts about your heritage, worried that you might have an affinity with sinister magic. Well, maybe now's a good time to be grateful to have an affinity with sinister magic.'

'I want to stay away from all of that.'

'How are you going to help her if you close your mind to it?'

'I'm not closing my mind.'

But he did need to think.

He returned to the reason he'd called Angelique in the first place. A family who had lost their magic; naja berries; the Oakmore Prophecy; impossible spells; terrible curses; and the disappearance of a teacher. He'd convinced himself it was all linked.

Cheery poked her head into the cupboard. 'Fancy a walk?'

'Not really.'

'You look like you need a walk, and the shop's empty – I can manage on my own.'

'I need to find a way to save my friend.'

'People are working on it.' She twirled Miss Young's stethoscope on her middle finger. 'Guess who forgot this. She won't feel proper without it.'

Seth reached for it reluctantly. 'All right. She visiting the twins on St Joanne's Walk again?'

Cheery shrugged. 'Expect so. You could call in and see them anyway; they've been proper sick. Number four, they live at.'

Seth set off, putting the stethoscope around his neck. It had two long pieces that went into your ears so you could listen to a patient's heartbeat. He'd love to hear the reassuring sound of Angelique's heartbeat right now, and know that he still had a chance to make things right. Just one more reason why he was desperate to visit Ward 23.

Nightshade slipped alongside him like a shadow. 'She *will* be all right.'

'You can't possibly know that. Inspector Pewter

wanted me to go home, Nightshade. You wanted me to go home. Wish I'd listened to you.'

'That wouldn't have stopped the apprentice attacks. The only way you're going to cure Angelique is if you solve this case, Seth,' she said, as they battled a sharp wind blustering through the narrow streets of Gramichee. A tin can rattled past them down the street.

Seth fiddled with Miss Young's fancy stethoscope as he walked, and felt a strange comforting sensation, a sucking motion, every time his hand closed over the end.

'Let's go over everything,' said Nightshade as they made a turn that took them to the bleak outskirts of the town. 'Reckon the answer's in your head somewhere.'

'We don't know anything, Nightshade,' said Seth glumly. 'It's just a muddle.'

Cheery had told him St Joanne's Walk was very close to St Joanne's Church. This was the first time he'd been here in daylight, and while the layout of the tree-lined road skirting the graveyard and little cottages was obviously much clearer, it was still a gloomy spot. It made him realize he and Cheery had been pretty lucky not to lose Calamus and spot him picking those naja berries. It felt like such a big clue, but a clue to what? He'd been convinced the naja berries were important.

'What happened to Dagger as a suspect?' went on Nightshade as they approached the row of cottages where the ill twins lived. 'You've forgotten about him because you feel guilty about his face. This is number four, so I'll leave you to it. And I don't think you've completely ruled out Calamus as a suspect either, have you? Keep thinking, Seth, you'll get there.'

Seth knocked, and when the door was answered he tried to hand the stethoscope to the tired woman who stood there. He muttered to her that Miss Young would need it. His mind was very busy and it took a second to tune into the surprise on the woman's face.

She dragged a hand through hair that didn't look as if it had been brushed in a week. 'Miss Young? She was ever so kind, called a few times, but that was a while ago now. I know everyone's a big fan of her potions and powders, but she wasn't making my little ones any better.'

Seth wasn't completely surprised to hear Miss Young's remedies hadn't been effective. Cheery hardly kept it a secret that she suspected Miss Young of being a fraud.

'In fact, I thought they were getting worse,' went on the woman. 'So I thought it wouldn't do any harm to ask Calamus to look in instead.'

This did surprise Seth, and it must have shown on his face, as the woman carried on quickly: 'I know what folk say about him, but soon as he treated them they perked up right away, started taking a bit of food.' Her face lit up unexpectedly with a smile. 'That's always a good sign, isn't it – when they start asking for food?'

Seth stared dumbly at the stethoscope in his hand. 'Miss Young isn't here?'

'No, pet. I told her not to bother, not since Calamus calls here every day. He's here every evening the minute he shuts up that shop.'

'Calamus calls here every evening? Right after work?'

The woman nodded.

'And he hasn't missed a visit?' Seth's mind was taking this in only slowly. He knew this was important. He really had been seeing things wrongly. Because that meant Calamus must have been here when Leaf Falling was attacked, exactly as he'd told Tendril.

Calamus had told Seth he'd lied to MagiCon only to protect his apprentice. And he'd been telling the truth. Finally, Seth knew without a doubt this meant he could rule out Calamus as a suspect. He could not be the Apprentice Assassin. He had an alibi.

Seth had come here with no idea beyond returning the stethoscope, but finally, he felt he was getting closer. Finally, he had to be on the path to discovering the truth and seeing things how they really were.

39. The Oakmore Prophecy

Seth's steps took him slowly back to the Belle Boutique, through the Forum, past the quiet cafe with its fluttering umbrellas. He walked slowly because his mind was racing.

Calamus had told the truth about visiting the sick twins. What else had Seth been looking at wrongly?

That meant the cloaked figure he'd followed to the graveyard could not be Calamus either, not if he went straight to visit the sick twins after work every day. So who was the cloaked figure? Seth groaned inwardly when he realized he'd never actually seen their face – their hood had been up the whole time.

Gramichee. Nightshade had told him nothing here was what it seemed.

Someone had been picking naja berries. Naja berries were in short supply. But Angelique had said naja berries would not put anyone to sleep – that they did the opposite, if anything. Another thing that seemed wrong. But everything was turning out to be the opposite of what he expected.

Why would anyone be picking them if they weren't commonly used in magic?

As he thought everything through, Seth had the glimmer of an idea. And then his feet started to race just as fast as his mind.

Folklore claimed naja berries made people appear younger or live longer, but that was said to be impossible magic. Yet to Seth, who struggled so much with getting his spells right, all magic seemed pretty impossible – and somehow that helped him to understand something.

He burst into the Boutique, the chimes clanging wildly, and went straight to rummage under the counter for one of the white boxes stashed there. The twins' mother said they got more ill when Miss Young visited. All along Cheery had said Miss Young was a fake and not at all magical. Was he finally starting to see things the right way around?

He took a white box from the main pile behind the counter. Miss Young had done something strange, he was only just remembering now. She had sold a different box to Mrs Squerr. One from *under* the counter. He stared at the two boxes. They were both labelled exactly the same. But were they identical?

He took packets from each pile into the kitchen prep area and got out two mixing bowls.

Cheery drifted in and stared. 'And what the hairy fishcakes are *you* doing?'

'I still have Miss Young's stethoscope, because she wasn't visiting the twins. She hasn't been for ages. I thought Calamus's story might break when I went there, but *he* visits there every day.'

Seth ripped open the first packet and shook the contents into a mixing bowl. Then he did exactly the same with one that had come from under the counter, emptying the powder into the other mixing bowl. He gave each a good sniff. Then he opened a few more packets, dividing them just as before.

'Have you gone completely nuts? We sell those for a fortune, you've just destroyed several bundles of cash in powdered form.'

Seth shoved first one bowl and then another

under Cheery's nose. 'Smell! I need to be sure.'

But he was already sure. His nose was telling him conclusively that they were not the same.

As he waited for Cheery, his fingers found the crumpled sheet of paper she had handed to him earlier. Angelique's notes – she'd written down details of the properties of naja berries and about the Oakmore Prophecy.

He read Angelique's words.

Oakmore Prophecy. One of the 'impossible' magics so beloved of fairy tales and folklore. Dubious legend relating to prolonging life, or even reversing ageing. Some books of folklore claim naja berries have magical potency related to cracking this one, so it is funny those two things have cropped up together. But no one's ever proved it. Would be banned magic if it worked, but just a myth.

'What am I supposed to be smelling?' snapped Cheery.

'Can't you tell the difference?'

'No. And she'll be back in a minute.' Cheery was looking worried now. 'I'll help you clear up.' The white powder drifting in the air was beginning to settle on everything.

'One smells completely different to the other. One has a light smell. And this one –' Seth lifted the second of the bowls – 'smells like wild garlic and limeflower.'

'And your point?'

'I've been looking at everything all wrong. We believed the sick twins at St Joanne's Walk were Miss Young's patients. We think her products aren't really magical. When the head of MagiCon came here, Miss Young didn't sell her one of the packets she sells to everyone else, she sold from a box under the counter. Why?'

Cheery frowned and sniffed both bowls again. 'All right, they might be two different products. I've always said she's a right old fraud. I guess the one she sold to Mrs Squerr might actually do something, so she can't be accused of peddling non-existent magic for a fortune?'

'That would mean there *is* something magical about the powder she sold to Kalinder Squerr.' Seth was lost in thought for a moment. 'But that really doesn't make sense. I know I've been looking at everything all wrong and I feel I'm close to seeing everything the right way round. Close.' He stared at the two bowls of powder. 'If she *can* do magic, why is she bothering to defraud people and selling non-magic stuff? And why didn't the twins get better when she visited?'

'Because we know Miss Young's got about as much magical power as the sausages I wish I'd had for my breakfast? But . . . OK, I really don't get it.'

'I think maybe I do.'

Cheery was shaking her head in confusion. 'There's nothing actually illegal about selling non-magical stuff that makes people feel better because they *think* it's doing them good, is there?'

'Then why be so careful to sell something different to the head of MagiCon? The only answer is because there is something very illegal about selling banned magic.'

Cheery had stopped giving anxious glances at the mess and now looked directly at Seth. 'What?'

'I think people are getting wise to the fact that Miss Young's Perfectly Prime Powders are not all they seem to be. But what if it's *not* because they don't do anything? What if we've been looking at it the wrong way?'

'You think her preparations are so popular because . . . ?'

'Granny Onabutter says she hasn't felt so sprightly in years. What if she's right? What if Miss Young isn't an innocent fraud, but . . . the opposite?' said Seth.

'You think she hasn't shown us anything of what

she's doing because she daren't? Because her preparations are secretly chock full of banned, sinister magic? You can't be serious.' Cheery looked half thrilled, half horrified. 'That's why she sold Mrs Squerr a different one? She had to sell one of the non-magical packets deliberately so she wouldn't get caught?'

'It's the only thing that makes sense,' said Seth. 'When you start to look at everything the right way. But why did the twins not get better? And how is she making all this powerful magic?'

Seth put the stethoscope on Cheery's cheek and it gently suckered it out of shape.

'Now you come to mention it, there are suddenly an awful lot of sick children in Gramichee,' said Cheery. 'Miss Young's a regular sight everywhere in the town looking after everyone.'

'The Oakmore Prophecy and naja berries,' Seth went on. 'They are both to do with impossible magic. Rejuvenation, extending life. I think it might take more than a few berries to reverse the ageing process. What if every time she goes out to visit young people, she's not curing them, but making them more ill?'

'Something with this?' Cheery took the stethoscope and began playing with it, letting it pucker her skin. 'I mean, I always said it wasn't really a stethoscope and she's not really a doctor.'

'Why are children becoming sleepy and ill? What if she's stealing something from them? What about if this stethoscope is how she steals a seriously dark and secret ingredient that makes her preparations so powerful?'

'She sucks something out of them?'

'What if it's a magical instrument she's using to suck out some of their life force? Why have people been struck with a Deathly Slumber? What if, sometimes, she takes too much and they do more than sleep?'

'On no. Don't think I can't see where this is going. Is this where your pea-sized brain has got you? You can't mean it. You think Miss Young is the Apprentice Assassin?'

40. She Can't Even Do Magic

'M iss Young?' sneered Cheery again. 'Come on!'
'I need to prove it,' said Seth.

'Well, good luck with that.' Cheery watched as he sniffed again at the two different bowls of powder. 'Stealing the souls of sick children? She can't even do magic, but now you suddenly think Miss Young is an incredible sorcerer who's cracked the legendary Oakmore Prophecy with the help of some sort of dark magical device?' She examined the stethoscope again. 'It's the sort of magic you could spend a lifetime researching and never find the answer. Miss Young's not even that old.'

'I agree it'd take years.'

Cheery winced. 'So . . . she arrives suddenly in Gramichee after secretly perfecting incredible magic somewhere.'

'And you'd probably need people to experiment on. Well, haven't we been looking for a link with a school?' said Seth thoughtfully.

'And she's, what – storing souls so she can add them to her magic? What – in a cupboard? And we just haven't noticed?'

The ancient boiler gave a trademark thunk.

Seth moved past her and down the corridor to the store cupboard. Miss Young would be back soon. He needed evidence.

Cheery followed, still challenging him, Seth still explaining.

'Stoney Warren was the home of a magical family, but it was turned into a school as their magic died out. A school for magical people would be a great place to hide for years and quietly experiment with banned magic – if anyone picked up on the odd trace of magic, they'd assume the kids had been mucking about.'

Cheery just looked at him as if he'd gone

completely insane. 'You going to go to Pewter with a mad theory and no evidence? Good luck with that.'

Seth reached to retrieve something from the cupboard – the hockey stick had been lying near where Angelique had been attacked. They'd simply tidied it away this morning, but Seth remembered he'd watched Miss Young take it from an ancient holdall when she'd put up his hammock. He'd noticed at the time it was stamped with an old school crest, but now he looked at the crest and recognized it. It was the Stoney Warren crest of two boxing rabbits.

He seized it in both hands. 'This is evidence it's not just a mad theory! Stoney Warren's crest! Miss Young must have sneaked up on Angelique looking at it. But even if she asked Miss Young a few uncomfortable questions, she wouldn't have known the dangers of letting that stethoscope anywhere near.'

He marched down the corridor, hockey stick in hand, until he was standing by the cellar door. He gave the door a shove. 'We need to get this open.'

'So how old is Miss Young really?' asked Cheery.

'Good question. And I've got several more. Why is this place overrun with mice? Why is the store-room always so hot? Why is the door to the cellar always locked? And why was Angelique attacked here, next to it?'

If Angelique were here she would effortlessly open this lock with her graceful magic. Not for the first time Seth cursed himself for still not being able to do any sort of useful magic, although ... He carefully placed the hockey stick on the floor so he was free to flex his fingers. Could he actually cause an explosion if he wanted to, rather than just accidentally? If the whole place burnt down he didn't really care – not if it saved Angelique.

Just as he started trying to channel his explosive tendencies, he felt a rush of air as Cheery launched herself past him, both aubergine-booted feet first, in a flying dropkick. The door splintered off its hinges in one go.

Cheery sprang back to her feet and rushed headlong down the dark cellar steps in front of him. He'd never seen her look so happy.

41. A ONCE IN A LIFETIME OFFER

Seth hadn't known what he expected them to find as they reached the bottom of the cellar steps. Cheery fumbled for a light switch and the low-ceilinged underground room was illuminated, and they discovered it was empty except for something at the far end, right underneath Seth's storeroom.

'What the heck is that?' whispered Cheery as they crept closer. The heat in the cellar was stifling.

That was a glass cylinder full of a bubbling pink liquid, almost completely wrapped in a rose-coloured blanket with a large thermometer stuck in one side. Like a sick child. For a moment, Seth thought it was alive.

'That's been down here all this time? What do we do with it? Kill it?' said Cheery, keeping her voice low, as if it could hear.

A mouse skittered past and made Seth jump. They both walked nervously right up to the glass jar sitting on the earth floor. Behind it was a series of pipes. One pipe, hot to the touch, wrapped around the tank under the blanket, keeping its contents artificially warm. Another came from inside the tank and had a tap on the end, which was off, but still leaking just a tiny dewdrop of liquid. If Seth was correct, a mouse was busy drinking a neat version of Miss Young's fulfilment of the Oakmore Prophecy magic directly from that leaky tap.

'Nightshade was right about the mice not being normal,' he muttered.

'I wonder just how many life forces she's stolen,' said Cheery, mesmerized by the softly bubbling pink liquid. She reached out towards the wall of the tank, but stopped short of touching it. 'Has Miss Young really put together a magical potion full of stolen souls? It looks more like an evil, glowing bubble bath.'

'That's the naja berries. At their most potent

when gathered at full moon,' said Seth. 'No wonder she keeps a clock where it's easier to follow the seasons of the moon than it is to tell the time. She must be growing them in secret in the graveyard.'

'That was never Calamus we were following at all? I suppose cloaked sinister sorcerers all look the same in dark graveyards, especially with their hoods up. But where is the missing teacher that Angelique has been investigating?'

Seth finally put his fingers on the warm jar, he could just feel the throb of the bubbles. ' Oh, I don't think Miss Young is just the Apprentice Assassin. I think the only answer that makes sense is that *she* is the teacher Angelique has been trying to trace. She's just been overdosing on her own potion. But can *we* use it?'

'Whaddayoumean?'

'It's obviously really powerful. If we could give it back to those who have had their life force stolen – do you think they'd wake up again?'

Cheery put her hands on her hips. 'I'd say take the whole thing to MagiCon so they can find out what to do with it. Plus, it's evidence. But I don't think we can lift it.'

'Oh, I don't think that will be necessary,' crooned a familiar voice behind them.

Cheery swung around, an annoyed look on her face. She wouldn't normally let someone sneak up on her like that. Seth turned more slowly, not quite able to take his eyes from that liquid, bubbling with vigorous stolen life.

'Sneaking down here? I put my trust in you two,' said Miss Young.

'We thought we could trust *you*,' retorted Cheery. 'Trust you not to steal the lives of the sick people you were supposed to be helping, and not to attack our friends.' She shifted a nervous glance at Seth. 'All to put into your preparations so you could make an enormous profit.'

'But it's not just benefiting me. Look how popular my preparations are. And I hardly pinch more than just a teensy sneak, just here and there.' Miss Young gently patted the glass tank snuggled up in its rose-coloured blanket. 'I've got so good at it, I can make an extraction in seconds, without people even noticing. Even in that busy corridor, even in among all those people bustling about when I snuck a little from Leaf,' she crowed.

'Now, my lovely apprentices.' She hiccupped softly and pressed her cheek against the glass container. 'We will never be in more high demand. I suppose I had to let you in on this some time. We are

314

fulfilling a need. This magic is unlike anything people have seen before. I will probably win an award! Let's do this – together!'

Cheery stepped closer to Miss Young. 'You think if people knew why they were so effective they would still buy 'em?'

Miss Young moved her cheek away. 'Oh yes, I do!'

'How do we switch it off?' demanded Seth, finally finding a voice. 'How do we return the life force to people?'

'Switch it off?' Miss Young swished her long curtain of red hair. 'Just because occasionally I get my quantities a teensy bit wrong? I've been working on perfecting this spell my whole life. Decades. And I have no intention of stopping, not now it's all finally going so perfectly. For years my only choice was to work as a teacher. Hardly more than a servant. And in the beautiful house that once belonged to my family! I was made to feel insignificant by all those superior girls – their sniggering and endless moaning about how unfair it was they *couldn't practise their marvellous magic*. I didn't mean any harm. It's just business.'

'Tell that to Armory Opal and Myrtle Rust. And Leaf's getting no better, and Angelique,' said Cheery, with another anxious glance at Seth.

'I did my best, but the demand! Oh, you don't know how exhausting it is, being so popular – all these dreary home visits, having to take just the tiniest sneaky pinch here and there. It was getting too slow. I really needed some supply. And Quartz Darkheart did go on about how she hated Armory Opal and how he'd made her principal to a girl from the wrong background – I was doing her a favour.' She smiled. 'But now there are three of us to collect ingredients, it's a relief, quite frankly. I am going to make you a once in a lifetime offer.'

'Armory Opal,' snapped Cheery. 'I told him you weren't teaching us because there was no magic in what you were doing, but his wife said your products were doing her good. Must've got him thinking it didn't add up. Do you know how that makes me feel about you killing him? It makes me feel responsible.' She inched closer to Miss Young.

Seth wondered how old Miss Young actually was. After all, she kept dosing herself with powders, smothering her skin in her various lotions. But Angelique had said Elfreda Oldcastle was supposed to have retired years ago. The magic she had invented must be incredibly powerful.

'Armory was very rude. Didn't understand at all. A destroyer of scientific magical advancement.

316

Wanting to wreck my life's work. There are always one or two casualties in the name of magical progress. All right, no more deaths! I promise.' She gave an awful smile. 'Join me! Goodness knows I need the help. You can both have shares in the business. All my hard-working years and you get it on a plate. Ten per cent of the business. Each. Do you know how much money that is?'

'Forget that. You are going to have to come along to MagiCon and explain yourself,' said Cheery, stepping aggressively closer to Miss Young, who backed off into a corner of the low, dark room.

Seth was only half listening. He cared far less about hauling Miss Young off to MagiCon to answer for her crimes than of getting hold of some of that precious liquid for Angelique. Could he siphon some off? How much would he need?

Miss Young looked at Cheery imploringly. 'Do you know how my family lost all their money? Because my great-uncle believed he could fulfil the Oakmore Prophecy. He spent every waking moment convinced it was possible. Worked his way through the family fortune. Everyone had him down as a fool. Then I came across his notes and I realized why he made all those sacrifices. He had been close.'

Miss Young crept back to kneel beside the glass jar, coddling it. 'I saw a chance to turn disaster into something good. And through trial and error and countless experiments, I did it. I worked for years! Seeking not just that spark of magic I felt sure was within me somewhere, but a glorious discovery. You won't stand in the way of me restoring the family fortune. It's my reward. My destiny.'

'Well, it's going to be a no from both of us,' said Cheery in a low but threatening voice. 'Miss Young, there are two of us. It's over. It might go better for you if you told us how to put those life forces back.'

That's when Seth noticed Miss Young's lethal stethoscope was looped around her neck – they must have left it upstairs.

'You drive a hard bargain. But, OK, fifty-fifty – twenty-five per cent for each of you.' Then, like a snake striking, she thrust the sucking end of the stethoscope towards Seth. 'Or you go in the jar.'

Seth took a step back towards the cellar steps, while Cheery stood her ground. There was a quavering voice behind him and he swirled around.

'Forever – are you all right? Are these apprentices ganging up on you? What's the meaning of all this?' Granny Onabutter was clutching her wicker basket and her thin lips were pressed together, her curranty eyes searching Cheery, Seth and Miss Young for an explanation.

'Silence.

'There was no one in the shop upstairs, so I thought I'd come and . . . Whatever it is you two are doing, stop it at once!'

Miss Young recovered first and stepped smartly towards Granny and escape, muttering 'thank goodness' and putting her shoulders back. But as she passed Cheery, a booted foot shot out and Miss Young went sprawling.

Granny stared open-mouthed at the principal lying face down on the dusty earth floor of the cellar. 'Well, it looks like I arrived just in time!'

'She's been stealing souls to put into magical preparations,' rattled out Cheery. 'She's been practising banned sinister magic, Granny Onabutter. Seth and I are taking her into MagiCon.'

'What nonsense,' snapped Miss Young, getting to her feet, her face flushed with intense anger as she dusted herself down. 'This is all the thanks I get for taking on two useless apprentices.'

No one moved. Granny Onabutter turned to Miss Young, her face crinkling. 'Not so fast, my dear, this is quite fascinating. Stealing souls, you say? Surely that's not even possible. Such advanced magic is only the stuff of legend.'

She put her head on one side as if she had all the time in the world and was contemplating a tricky clue in a crossword puzzle. 'But do you know, I always wondered. Those powders. So very expensive. But I've never felt so sprightly in years. I think there might be something in what they are saying.'

'Miss Young's killed people,' went on Cheery. 'We think she's attacked countless others for years as she's perfected her spell. Miss Young is the Apprentice Assassin.'

Granny Onabutter took out her half-finished knitting and removed a length of wool from the needles.

'Well, that sounds like some very sinister magic,' she muttered, shaking her head. 'Finding a way of stealing the souls of all those apprentices flooding our little Gramichee.'

She held out her knitting needles, one in each hand, and as she crossed them across her chest they crashed with the clang of heavy metal and grew instantly into long spears.

She bent her knees into an attack pose and held one spear to Cheery's throat, while Seth felt the other press into the skin of his own neck. 'Fifty-fifty shares in the business, did you say, my dear Miss Young?'

'You have *got* to be kidding me,' said Cheery.

42. IT'S YOUR DESTINY

Cheery, swift as lightning, kicked Granny in the knee, taking her by surprise and giving her time to dodge as Granny Onabutter jerked the spear upwards, narrowly missing slicing through Cheery's throat. Cheery's CWK classes had made her too agile – she went for Granny's wrist and flipped her on to the dirt floor.

Seth didn't hesitate. While Miss Young was watching in horror as Granny Onabutter went flying, still clinging to her threatening spears, Seth grabbed the stethoscope.

They wrestled with it as Granny righted herself, staggered and, her face set with grim determination, advanced on Cheery, who was left looking about wildly for something to defend herself with the points of both spears were thrust towards her.

The jar carried on bubbling joyfully. Seth, seeing Cheery in trouble, abandoned his tug of war and tossed her the only other thing in the almost bare room – Granny Onabutter's wicker knitting basket.

Cheery caught it in one hand and aimed it at the side of Granny's head – the old lady fended off the blow with one spear and struck with the other. The point went through the basket but snagged on a thick ball of speckly green wool inside, otherwise it would have pierced Cheery right through the heart.

Granny Onabutter gave an evil smile.

Miss Young turned to Seth and began to wheedle: 'You understand, you'll join me, won't you Seth? I knew your mother, you know. You are the last in a very long line of very talented sorcerers and I can help you claim your true heritage.

'No one thought I possessed any magical ability at all. I was written off. But I was convinced I had something, just a spark – and that's enough, if you work hard enough. And I did work hard. I've achieved something brilliant.' She went on and on in a coaxing voice. 'Together we'd be magnificent. We could run the world. No one could stop us. This is what your mother would have wanted. Seize control of your power.'

The fear inside him was mixed with anger. He wanted to cover his ears to blot out the words. But Cheery was backed into a corner and he was frozen with the horror of it all.

'I did choose an apprentice from a non-magical family to steal from. Life force was so strong in her.' Forever moved close enough to breathe conspiratorially in his ear. 'Non-magical heritage, not like you. You are one of us. Magic should be allowed to be powerful. We'll restore our family fortunes together.'

'No! I am training to become a sorcerer to fight people like you!' Seth heard himself yelling, stepping away from Miss Young.

Cheery was dancing and dodging to keep out of the way of Granny Onabutter's spears but Seth knew they were going to lose this battle.

Angelique would not survive.

The thought made him stop backing away. He would never give up on Angelique. Miss Young was going to have to do her worst.

But Granny Onabutter was suddenly in front of

him too, having side-stepped away from Cheery. He was trapped. The point of a spear pressed into the skin of his neck once again. Cheery was pinned to the back wall by the point of the second spear – even with her martial arts training, she wasn't going to fight her way out of this one. When he'd been in a tight corner before, Angelique had always managed to come to his rescue. But that wasn't going to happen.

But it wasn't that which really made him despair.

It was Miss Young, who just went on pleading. 'Your mother understood that the best magic always goes to the most powerful. That's you, Seth – you could rise to greatness if you would only stop messing about trying to do wishy-washy happy magic. It's not you, Seth. It's not your path, it's not your destiny.'

'Need any more life force to add to your wonderful spell?' suggested Granny Onabutter. 'I'll hold them back, you do what needs to be done.'

Miss Young reached for her stethoscope and advanced first on Cheery. Granny lifted the spear point out of the way, but that was all Cheery needed. In the blink of an eye, she flashed out a hand, grabbing the spear, and kicked Miss Young in the stomach. Granny lost her grip and there was a clash of metal on metal as they fought with the enormous knitting needles, clashing again and again in a dance around the low-ceilinged cellar.

Seth seized his chance to do the only thing he could think of. He fumbled to untie the soft rose-pink blanket from around the jar.

'No!' cried Miss Young, getting back to her feet and grabbing at Seth. 'Don't destroy it!'

But that was the last thing he wanted. He needed that life force to bring Angelique back. His plan had been to get behind Granny Onabutter and smother the blanket over her head.

But she was on to him and spun around, tearing his tunic with the point of her spear, narrowly missing making a slice in his stomach. Seth had missed his chance.

He was despairing of anything that could possibly help them when two small shapes, hissing and spitting, rushed in. Nightshade and Gorgeous Tom hurled themselves, claws unsheathed, into the fight.

The two women tried to kick back, but Gorgeous Tom looked as if he was enjoying himself, stalking Granny Onabutter, dodging her kicks and spear jabs. A small smear of blood stained the orange fur of his chin – Seth didn't think it was the cat's.

Nightshade turned her big green eyes on him. 'I finally worked it out when I saw her heading after you. She –' hissed Nightshade, pointing a paw at Granny Onabutter – 'comes from an old magical family that's ashamed of their lack of magical ability. She's too embarrassed to even call herself Troutbean any more. Onabutter is an anagram of Troutbean. Worked that out myself. Told you nothing in Gramichee was what it seemed.'

Seth didn't have time to worry that Nightshade had been so keen to show off her cleverness, she'd forgotten not to talk. But Cheery just laughed. 'You mean her granddaughter is the famously non-magical Gloria Troutbean?'

With an angry ginger furball to help, Cheery was finally winning, forcing Granny backwards until Cheery's spear hovered threateningly at Granny's throat. 'The one who no one would take on as an apprentice? Seth, tie her up with her own knitting.'

But Miss Young wasn't finished yet. 'I know what your mother was,' she said to Seth. 'When I taught her I could see it in her, the darkness. And I see it in you. Look what she became. Welcome it in!'

Nightshade sprang at her, but Miss Young grabbed the cat by the scruff of the neck and hurled her across the room. Nightshade hit the cellar wall with a sickening crack.

Her prone body slumped down on the dirt floor and she didn't so much as twitch a whisker, not even when a mouse ran right over her soft pink nose.

43. The Rage Within

There was a yowl of anguish from Gorgeous Tom.

Miss Young loomed over Seth. 'You've no parents, no friends, and now not even your cat. You may as well join me.'

'Tie her up, Seth!' called Cheery desperately, as Granny thrust her remaining spear wildly, trying to resist being pinned against the wall.

Rage swirled into a storm within Seth. He could feel fury crackling through him, a fizzing that filled his insides with electricity. He felt white hot. As he lifted his hands to push Miss Young out of his way so he could get to his cat, two balls of flame erupted from them, jets of fire blasting from his fingers.

Miss Young sidestepped and narrowly dodged the flames, which carried on and struck the glass jar with the force of a rocket. There was a crack and a giant splintering and then the entire vessel exploded.

They all ducked and covered their heads as tiny shards of glass flew across the cellar. The pink liquid shot outwards in a beautiful cascade, then eagerly formed foaming rivulets on the dirt floor.

Seth watched in absolute horror. His only plan to save Angelique and the others was to use some of that precious liquid. Instead, he had exploded it.

He rushed to Nightshade and dug his fingernails into the bubbling dirt, desperately trying to stop all of the liquid from being lost. He cupped his palm and dribbled a tiny amount of the precious liquid into the side of Nightshade's mouth. Her immobile body was like a dark puddle on the floor. He told himself she was just injured, hoped that she would get up any second and say something annoying.

Seth heard a scream of protest. It filled his ears, but he ignored it. He focused on scraping what liquid he could salvage into Nightshade's mouth.

But then another piercing scream dragged his

gaze up. He watched in horror as dark splodges grew all over Miss Young's usually flawless skin. The smoothness of her face was turning to wrinkles. The skin on her arms becoming baggy and creased. Her long, luscious red hair was turning brittle. Seth remembered with a jolt how frequently she used her own preparations.

She held the backs of her decaying hands out in front of her, examining them with a look of terror. The dark splodges blossomed, skin growing saggier, her hair became the colour of straw, then thin and white. Her face was ageing by the second –from the confident one Seth knew, to that of an unfamiliar old woman.

Cheery and Granny Onabutter were no longer fighting, transfixed by the horrifying spectacle of Miss Young growing old in front of their eyes. And still she kept ageing. Her face seemed to cave in, and a few teeth fell out.

Seth just kept on kneeling by Nightshade, desperately trying to feed her the very last drops of the pink liquid, hoping to see her tongue dart out. But she remained motionless. He tried to shut out what was happening to Miss Young – she was now bent, withered, her head almost bald with just a few tufts of white hair left.

Miss Young staggered right up to him, looking like something that had been dug up in the graveyard of St Joanne's. She stretched her hands towards him, grasping hold of his tunic. He looked at the ancient hand gripping him with revulsion. She stumbled closer, her eyes blind and milky. She put her face close to his and opened her empty mouth in a long scream.

Her terrified screech filled the cramped room, and her grasping hands appeared more like ancient branches as she continued to shrivel and to age. Her whole body became grey and cracked until she got smaller and drier and shrivelled completely to dust, finally disintegrating into nothingness.

Cheery was the first to move, not giving Granny the chance to react before lifting the spear against her neck.

'Well, I don't think anyone would want any of Miss Young's powders after that,' said Cheery.

Seth rose to help tie up Granny Onabutter. The knitting basket and one long spear were abandoned on the ground amid a crystalline sparkle of broken glass. The remains of the pink liquid were no more than dark stains on the floor. Every trace of the life-force it contained was gone.

There was a shuffle of footsteps down the cellar

steps. Seth turned to see the imposing figure of Inspector Pewter ducking to enter the low basement room, followed by Dagger Tourmaline.

'What did I miss?' Pewter said. His gaze fell on Seth and then Nightshade. Without a further word, he gently lifted the black cat and carried her body away.

44. Unlicensed Magic

Seth waited in the shadow of the dragon curtain, after having once more slipped into the curorium the back way.

Calamus's familiar white-hair was bent over one of his ancient spell books. He stirred a spoon in a cup of tea. He might not even have moved since Seth was last here.

'I hope you are not here to try to persuade me to try unlicensed magic,' Calamus said, without turning, after Seth had been standing there a little while.

He'd been hesitating what to say, but decided to tell him everything that had just happened in the cellar, from Miss Young's years spent perfecting a terrible spell that only worked because she stole the life force from people, to the destruction of the spell.

'I'd hoped if we could give those who have had their life force stolen from them a large enough dose of Miss Young's spell, we might be able to reverse the process.'

'But that spell is now soaked into the ground?' Calamus nodded. 'So your bright idea is to feed experimental magic to those poor souls who are in Ward 23? What do you think the consequences might be of that?' The way Calamus put it did make it sound stupid and reckless. But that was exactly what Seth was going to propose. He felt he had no choice. 'If we do nothing, they'll die. Anyway, it's not experimenting if you help me – you know so much.' He had to take the risk to save Angelique. 'The spell is based on the Oakmore Prophecy – it's supposed to give you a long life. Miss Young managed to create a powerful enough spell to actually reverse ageing. You mentioned that prophecy to me when I brought you that list. If we start with the magical ingredients Miss Young was using,' Seth pressed on, 'we could invent a spell that's close.'

Seth waited. He knew it was a slim hope. But Calamus was so skilled, there had to be a chance. Calamus reached thoughtfully for one of his ancient old grimoires and flicked through its crusty pages. Seth dared to hope he was looking for ideas for a spell. Or was he simply hinting he thought Seth should leave?

'Foolhardy optimism.'

'You're the only one who can help me,' pleaded Seth. 'We know the basic ingredients.'

'The most powerful sorcerer in the world cannot help poor Armory Opal or Myrtle Rust.'

'But you think we can do something for the others?' Seth asked quickly, seizing this smallest of hints.

Calamus croaked on in his low, weak voice. 'I hope you are not suggesting that I dabble in the sinister arts, young man.'

'But that *is* how you cure cursed people, isn't it – you have to know the spell that was used. So it's only reversing a spell. I can't see that it's wholly sinister magic. Anyway, I'm not asking you to do a spell at all. I'll be the one doing the magic.'

'You? You think you can do that dubious magic and reverse it?'

'I can't do it alone. But I'm willing to try.'

Calamus leant closer to the page, a yellow finger tracing the details of a spell. 'When you brought me that list I was suspicious that someone was trying to fulfil the Oakmore Prophecy. That is old and powerful magical lore. I had my suspicions of Miss Young. I admit I was intrigued. Particularly as Miss Young's natural magical ability was weak. Yet she managed such impressive magic. I couldn't help wonder if she'd managed to crack it, purely for reasons of study and professional curiosity, of course.'

Seth said nothing. He just held his breath and hoped.

'But it's probably wrong to be impressed by such a thing, especially as it appears the minute she cracked it, she couldn't resist setting up shop in Gramichee making an awful lot of money. Our biggest problem might be that Miss Young has greedily snatched up the supplies of naja berries.'

'Our biggest problem? You mean . . . wait, have you been working on a cure already? Since I brought you that list? You're going to help me?' Seth allowed himself to hope. 'Could you do a healing spell if we had some naja berries?'

'We might have tried. But I have already checked St Joanne's graveyard, where it seems Miss Young was collecting her supply. All gone. Such was the demand for her products. We will have to wait until we can source some more.'

But Seth could not wait. It had already taken him way too long to see things as they really were – and that had endangered Angelique. 'So if I had naja berries, you'd help me?' Seth was already out of the door. 'I'll be right back.'

It took him a little while to climb up to Granny Onabutter's balcony via the criss-crossing metal fire escape. Or Granny Troutbean, as he thought of her now. Who would have thought that when he'd persuaded Ten to move those sickly plants up to the balcony that they would turn out to be so crucial.

A few minutes later, he handed over the berries, his hands stained with their faint pinkish glow. Calamus's gaze and his heavily lidded eyes went to the window.

'It's a day past full moon. They won't be as potent.'

'Well,' Seth breathed hard. 'Perhaps we can compensate by putting more life force into the spell, just like Forever Young did.'

'That is definitely banned sinister magic, Seth Seppi,' rapped Calamus. 'All those poor youngsters who unwillingly gave their life force to make older people young. It is against the natural order of things.'

'I wasn't going to suggest using anyone else's.' Seth took the stethoscope from beneath his blue tunic and held it out nervously. The sinister object had been abandoned in the confusion in the cellar, as Dagger Tourmaline and Cheery had wrestled Granny up the stairs. 'We'll use mine.'

When Pewter had carried Nightshade away, Seth had known there was nothing more he could do for his beloved friend. But he could still help Angelique and Leaf. He placed Miss Young's stethoscope on the pitted workbench alongside the grimoire Calamus had been poring over. They had to use it before someone realized an object of such darkly sinister magic had gone missing.

'You want to give your life because you think it will save your friend? Noble sentiment, but I don't think it will even be that easy. You can't control it. It's too dangerous. I cannot agree.'

'You have to agree. Because I will do it on my own if you don't help. Then I really will have no idea how to control how much of myself to put into the spell. Last time, I collapsed without even using this.' He pushed the evil object nearer to Calamus.

His clawed yellow nails poked at it. 'I should waste time pointing out the extreme danger of what you are suggesting, I suppose. This is magic beyond my experience. You trust me to extract your life force?'

'If you'll trust me enough to do magic with someone who has done so little successfully. I usually blow things up.'

Seth thought of the terrible effects of magic. Of people growing ancient and then crumbling to dust. Could he possibly believe he could do this? So far, his magic had been useless. The only spell he'd managed to get right had been a bad one.

He tried to shut his mind to the poisonous words Forever Young had dripped into his mind while they had been in that terrifying cellar. But he knew they'd haunt him always. All those terrible accusations about his magical heritage and future.

Calamus had told him he had a power. Well, he may as well try to use it.

'Angelique is my friend,' he pleaded. 'You can't stop me doing this, but I've more chance of succeeding with your help.' He felt his magical future was beyond repair anyway.

Calamus was pressing parts of the stethoscope, putting his nose close to it.

'I wouldn't dream of stopping you! I'm utterly fascinated to see what happens.' He smiled, his puckered skin crumpling like tissue. 'Purely for reasons of study and curiosity, of course. It would be very easy to kill you, you know. Although,' he put his aged head to one side, 'it would be very much easier to kill myself if I offered to do it for you. I'm an old man. So. Shall we get on?'

He smoothed a page where a spell was already written. He really had taken that list of ingredients and studied it. Perhaps he had listened when Pewter had asked for his help all along.

Calamus added the naja berries to a row of ingredients already assembled at the back of the workbench, as if anticipating this moment.

Seth looked at the lethal stethoscope that had been used to kill Myrtle Rust and Armory Opal and could not stop a dry chuckle. 'If this is sinister magic, I can probably make it work,' he joked weakly, in a vain attempt to cover his nervousness. 'But . . . you're already in trouble from having done sinister magic in the past. Will this get you in more trouble if you help me?'

Calamus shrugged. 'Good and evil magic. Some folk like to think it's as simple as that. But there are those who believe it's less to do with the magic you practise than the sort of sorcerer you are, and what *you* put into it.' He lifted the stethoscope. 'Let's hope I don't do anything too bad, then, for both our sakes.

Now, it's not exactly the time I would have chosen for your first lesson in magic, but as you do this, remember, you can't command magic – you have to reach inside of you. You have to ask for it.'

Seth was finally getting a lesson that somehow seemed to speak to him. Typical that he would be getting it now. He answered with a swift nod before he could think; before he could take too much notice of the cold sweat prickling down his back. All he thought of was Angelique.

The elderly curologist waved his hand across the dim lamplight pooling on to the table in front of him. The light responded instantly by glaring brightly.

Seth was always amazed at how effortless some people made doing magic seem. He never tired of seeing it happening in front of him. It sent a shiver the full length of his spine.

'And I need to bottle three doses of whatever spell you think will wake everyone up,' he said.

'Three.' Calamus's only other response was to place three tiny glass bottles with gold stoppers on the workbench and again smooth the page in front of him where he had made notes in his spidery hand.

'Will extracting enough for three kill me?' Seth asked, failing to keep the fear from his voice.

Calamus scratched his head. 'You adorn me with greater knowledge than I have. You won't want my answer, which is *let's hope not*. Maybe I could take four – one for myself as a reward? I too might like to be young again.'

Seth looked at him, horrified, until Calamus started trembling with laughter. 'Only joking, young Seth. Now – let us begin.'

'And you will try to stop if you think I might be dying?'

Calamus's burnt face leered over him. Seth suddenly felt dizzy, and his knees were buckling underneath him. Once again Angelique's familiar warning flashed through his brain: *You have a terrible habit of trusting the wrong people.*

45. MAKING ANY DIFFERENCE

The room smelt of the freshly laundered white sheets that were tucked up right under his chin. He was in a hard, narrow bed in a silent, white-painted room he had definitely never been in before. White curtains at the window were drawn, so he could see nothing outside. Had he . . .

Was he dead?

Or had he survived whatever spell he'd colluded on with Calamus? If so, had it worked?

He felt kind of OK, but the moment he tried to

move his legs, he changed his opinion about that. It felt as if weights were pressing down on him as he struggled to sit up. He forced his legs over the side of the bed, fumbling his feet on a cold hard floor. He needed to know. If he wasn't dead, then had the spell worked? Had his dangerous idea made any difference?

A discrete grey door in the corner opened softly and in walked his answer. 'Are you trying to get up? That's good,' said Angelique, sidling up to the bed.

'This isn't a dream, is it?' Seth replied. He probed the back of his head, which was aching. 'I feel a bit . . . there's a lump.'

She perched on the end of the bed. 'Yes, well, you're lucky it's just a lump on the back of your head.' She punched him on the arm hard enough that it hurt more than his head. 'Calamus told us everything, you know. I'm not sure whether to say thank you or tell you off for taking such a stupid risk.'

'You're awake. And I'm not dead! Why don't you just go with your first idea and say thank you.'

'I'd have been absolutely fine.' She stuck her long nose in the air, then she threw her arms around him in such a hug it hurt even more than the punch. 'You shouldn't have done it! Nobody's ever done anything like that for me, ever.'

'But you've rushed to my rescue plenty of times. If

it made a difference, I'm glad I did what I did. I only wish I could have saved Nightshade,' Seth added in a small voice.

Angelique turned away, looking towards the door, as if she couldn't even look at him. 'The thing is, Seth, that spell of Forever Young's really was strong. Even a few dirty drops might have . . .'

Then, as if he'd been hovering outside just waiting for this cue, in walked Inspector Pewter cradling a soft bundle of black fur in his arms.

'Nightshade!'

Seth tried to struggle out of bed, but his weariness was so overwhelming he just reached out his arms, and Pewter placed Nightshade into them. She snickered and snuggled into him. 'First cat ever in Ward 23!' she said proudly. 'Not that they gave me a proper bed. The talking thing might be a bit more out the bag, by the way.'

Seth just kept stroking her, and she began to purr like a kettle coming to the boil.

'Just under my left ear there, Seth, that's right.'

'This is Ward 23? Did Calamus use Miss Young's device on me for too long? Is that why I'm here?'

Seth had a sudden fear that he had lost weeks or even months of his life. Years? He had known there would be consequences, he just hoped they wouldn't all come too quickly. 'How long have I been asleep for?'

'Since last night,' sniffed Angelique.

'That magic you stupidly got Calamus to do wasn't what put you out,' explained Nightshade. 'You fainted, keeled over backwards and hit your head. You were out cold for a while, and then we let you sleep off the worst of the headache. You really are still rubbish at doing magic, you know, even though you've apparently actually done something good.'

Good? Hadn't Seth openly used a banned spell?

'Now I know you're all right,' went on Nightshade, 'and before you expect me to come rushing along to do something else that's risky or will involve me being carried about in a basket, Gorgeous Tom wants to show me the sights of Gramichee. Personally, I don't think it'll take long, but if you're going to be lying around all day . . .'

'Thought you called him Useless Tom?' said Seth, ruffling her fur. 'Thought you hated Gramichee.'

'I'm big enough to change my mind.'

'And what about Leaf?' Seth looked directly at Inspector Pewter. 'What's going to happen to Ten? And Dagger? And how is Cheery? She was brilliant, you know.'

'Well, young Vetch's fleekies attack on Dagger

can't be overlooked, but a transfer to an apprentice-ship away from Gramichee is the most likely outcome.'

'Not too far I hope, I'd like to see him again, I'm sure he only tricked me because he was under so much pressure.'

'You *will* trust all the wrong people,' said Angelique, rolling her eyes. 'He's not the only one changing apprenticeships. What with everything that's happened, and Red Valerian still being at large, my mother has decided MagiCon could use another trainee – Cheery seemed like a perfect fit. She'll probably dropkick me for telling you, but she was terribly worried about you, Seth.'

'We all were,' said Pewter. 'Despite your rash insis-tence on doing some very sinister magic indeed, and putting yourself in such peril, you have survived. As has Leaf Falling – she is presently sitting up and demanding second breakfast. It's mostly down to the remarkable abilities of Calamus – that you didn't die, that is. Not that I'd have gone ahead with your idea in the first place.'

Which was precisely why Seth had not gone to the inspector. 'It worked. And Nightshade? How did she...? I thought, I thought...'

'Giving her some of that spell of Miss Young's before it soaked into the floor,' said Pewter. 'That was quick thinking. Made all the difference, according to Dr Meanwell. Don't think he's ever had a furry patient before.'

'Then it was all worth it. Even if I'm banned from ever using magic ever again.' No one said anything, and Seth picked at the sheet covering him. 'For some reason, I only seem to be able to do sinister sorcery. I know that's bad,' he admitted. He'd get used to the fact that his magical future was in tatters. In time. Well, he'd have to. The important thing was that Angelique and the others were fine. As Pewter had said to him very recently, there were things more important than magic.

Pewter leant forward with his usual unreadable expression. Was he going to be arrested? 'Calamus didn't use that infernal contraption of Miss Young's on you at all.'

'Then how come you both recovered if none of my life force has been taken from me?' he asked Angelique, who surprised him by reaching forward and plucking a single hair painfully out of Seth's head.

'Calamus is an incredibly skilled sorcerer. He saved you from doing something very rash. You did incredible magic, Seth. Apparently this confirms what all of us suspected.' Angelique held the hair up to the light. 'A spell is only as strong as the person casting it. Miss Young had barely a glimmer of true magic and had to go to enormous lengths to get any of her magic to work, but once you'd fainted, Calamus just used three hairs from your head. You are one powerful sorcerer.'

Seth felt a familiar rush of hope, knowing he was still clinging on to his cherished dreams of one day being an incredible sorcerer. He had to learn to get over that.

'Do I get charged with something?'

He guessed he knew the answer. The Elysee would hardly overlook the fact he'd openly performed banned magic.

'Carry on with this risky magic and you will be charged with something,' warned the inspector sternly, his eyes glowing a particularly intense shade of blue. 'But not today.'

Seth felt relief rush out of him. 'Thank you.' He guessed Pewter must have pulled a few strings. And Mrs Squerr. But was he really in the clear?

'It wasn't just the sinister magic I did with Calamus – I made the fleekies spell and I practically blew someone up,' admitted Seth. 'Are you going to arrest me for that?' He looked at the tidy chest of drawers beside the bed, and with another urgent thought, fumbled about in the top drawer. Had Calamus kept his promise and produced a third phial of the recovery spell?

'You do seem to be very keen that I arrest you for something,' said Pewter, his eyes gleaming blue behind his glasses. 'You are not dead, young Seth. And Glad Tidings tells me she will have the world's biggest trickerchockerglory all ready for you.'

'You blew up a glass jar containing a terrible spell, Seth,' Angelique said. 'Miss Young blew herself up by smothering herself in banned magic.'

Something *was* in the cabinet. It was small, flat and rectangular, coloured red and didn't look in the least bit remarkable. But Seth recognized what it was, and even holding it brought all his dreams rushing in. He reluctantly held it out to Inspector Pewter.

'Someone's left their Elysee library card here.'

Pewter stared at it, as if he'd never seen one before. As if he'd never seen one of these magical cards grow and turn into a magical version of the library so that you could borrow a book wherever you might be.

'Calamus tells me your most urgent training should be in reining yourself in; not putting too much of yourself into your magic,' said Pewter. 'And I'd say it might be useful to learn how not to fall badly when you keel over. You could have learnt a lot from him. Shame that scamp Vetch has put him off apprentices. Now, your Prospect, about that—'

The inspector was interrupted by the door opening to admit the same short, white-coated figure with a very round, very red face who had taken away Herb Camphor when he'd been struck by the rebound of his own rock.

He bustled over to Seth's bedside, over-large hands flapping like a bird, and looked accusingly at Pewter and Angelique. 'Well, what are you all here for? We told you no more than one visitor at a time and no more than three minutes each – and, wait – that dratted *cat* is here?'

'They *are* very clean, cats, but apologies, Dr Meanwell,' soothed Pewter, extracting Nightshade even though she used her claws to try to cling to the bedsheet.

Dr Meanwell was looking at Seth. 'Are you ready?'

'For what?'

'Apparently you enquired about another patient. We are about ready to receive visitors, but we really must insist this is for a very short time indeed. We have to put our patients first.'

'Of course, Dr Meanwell,' replied Pewter, offering Seth an arm to help him out of bed. 'I thought you quite wanted to see your mother.'

46. MAGICAL DETOX

'S he's awake?' asked Seth, hardly daring to believe it as he followed the short, quick steps of Dr Meanwell and the long strides of Inspector Pewter along a squeaky-floored corridor that reminded Seth quite a lot of the Elysee HQ. 'She's finally recovered?'

'We said she was ready to receive visitors,' snapped the crotchety-faced doctor. 'She's been in a harsh magical curse for a long time and it's going to take more than a few weeks for her body to rid itself of all that sinister magic.'

A couple of corridors later they stopped outside a small window screened by dull grey curtains.

'Is this still Ward 23?' asked Seth.

'Well, of course it is,' barked the doctor. 'Where did you think it was, Santa's workshop?' He pressed a button next to the window and the grey curtains began to slowly fold back on themselves to reveal a tiny room, not with a bed in it, but a bath full of what looked like mud. It was not what Seth expected.

But then what had he expected? Certainly not to see a sleeping face poking out above the brown-grey sludge. A face Seth could just recognize as his mother's. Seth put his hand on the glass.

'Can I go in and talk to her?'

'We doubt she'll hear you. As you insisted you wanted to see her, we've had to put her under a stillness enchantment. Not a strong one – the last thing she needs is someone casting a load of spells over her. Her body is still trying to free itself of one particularly nasty spell.' Dr Meanwell sounded exceedingly cross, but then relented. 'But seeing as you've freed up a few beds, we don't see why not.'

He unlocked the door and Seth stepped nervously up to the bath. 'Has she— Can I—?'

With a sigh, Dr Meanwell reached into the mud and with a slurping, sucking sound pulled an arm free. 'The very finest mud from Our Glorious Swamp. Best thing for magical detox. Don't keep it out too long,' he said, placing the hand in Seth's.

Seth wrapped his fingers around his mother's.

'You've already put her recovery back with that stillness charm we've had to conjure over her.' The doctor pursed his lips and muttered something about mixing magic. 'Well, you wouldn't have wanted to see her before. Never seen someone so disturbed. Screaming was terrible, and noxious magic coming off her in clouds. We had complaints from the other patients.' He gave an unexpectedly kind smile. 'But this mud is very soothing. Good idea of mine.'

Seth felt the damp warmth of his mother's hand. He began to speak to her in a low, quiet voice, telling her that she would get well and all the things he'd like to talk to her about. He told her about the trophy he'd seen.

Elfreda Oldcastle had been at Stoney Warren her whole life. In that terrible cellar she'd gone on about how she knew his mother and had taught her.

Would his mother remember her? Oldcastle must have been experimenting for years. Hadn't

Angelique mentioned incidents of girls sleeping a lot? He would love to know what his mother knew. But like all the many questions he'd like to ask, that one would have to wait.

It looked as if he'd dodged for now any consequence of the sinister magic he had done. But would he ever pass his Prospect and be allowed into the Elysee library to find out anything about his mother's background? He would just have to wait until she awoke and they could talk properly, he told her.

At least she looked peaceful. Every now and again a small spiral of coloured gas puffed up from the mud with a soft pop. Seth wondered if this was the magical curse gradually being released from her body. If so, it meant she was getting better.

As Seth talked, for just one tiny moment, he thought he felt his hand being squeezed back. But the pressure was so slight, he wasn't completely sure he hadn't imagined it.

He was aware that Pewter had shuffled Dr Meanwell out of the room, despite a lot of protestations. He knew he wouldn't have long and hoped for just another squeeze, maybe a flicker, for her eyes to open, for there to be a sign telling him she was all right and knew he was there for her when she awoke.

'Dr Meanwell is a total genius at magical recovery.

Once he knows a spell he'll work at unpicking the effects for as long as it takes.' Pewter stuck his hands deep into the pockets of his suit – his trademark silvery one, rather than the boring navy one he'd been wearing recently. 'Of course his bedside manner is appalling. Don't worry about any of what he says about your mother. She's in the best hands.'

Seth felt Pewter's warm grip on his shoulder. In the cellar, when Miss Young had been going on and on about his mother, she'd said *look what she became* . . . Well, what exactly had she become?

The question was on the tip of his tongue when Pewter slipped a hand into a pocket and passed Seth something. He looked at the small glass bottle with a gold stopper. The third of the phials.

'I am giving you this, Seth, despite my better judgement.'

Seth stared at the last remaining phial of the recovery spell. 'Do you think this would work on her?'

'I think that it would almost definitely wake her.' Pewter dug both hands deep into his silver suit. 'Because you have not been arrested, it's worth reminding you that phial contains banned magic. Or at least what everyone except the most enlightened will see as sinister magic. I can see why you were so tempted to use your talents for this. But it's a path

I very much hope you will never go down again. However, as you risked so much to get it, it's yours, but can I offer some advice?'

Seth nodded as he tucked the precious phial away in one of his endless pockets, still hoping for a sign that his mother knew he was there.

'That's not the main reason I don't want you to use it,' said Pewter. 'It's not the sleep that she needs to be cured of. She's being kept in a magically enhanced state in the hope she will come out the other side unharmed. Now is not the time to call on this magic that you were willing to risk your life for. For now, Seth, leave it to the experts. Anyway, I expect you will be rather busy.'

Pewter passed something else over to Seth. In his palm was the red Elysee library card that Seth had found in the bedside cabinet. 'This was left here by Count Marred.'

'Count Marred came to visit me himself? While I was asleep? What did I do to deserve a visit from the new Sorcerer General?' That sounded like big trouble.

'This card was left behind by Count Marred, but it isn't his. It's yours.'

For the first time since setting his eyes on his mother, Seth lifted them away from her for more than a few seconds to look directly at the inspector.

'Mine? But you only get one of these when you pass your Prospect.'

'Indeed. That is what the Sorcerer General would have told you had you not been asleep when he came to pay you a call and to award you with this most desired and treasured of objects. But no matter, I'm sure you can say your thanks next time you see him.'

Seth opened and shut his mouth, but he had so many questions he simply didn't know where to begin.

Luckily Pewter went on to explain. 'You proved you can do magic to an Elysee Prospect Committee official. Calamus was there to witness you demonstrating more than just the necessary spark of magic.'

'Calamus is . . . but I thought—'

'He very kindly assists as a Prospect judge. The Sorcerer General approved of bending the rules just a little. I had to help with the paperwork. You made it, Seth! Sounds like you have performed magic a couple of times now, if of a rather dubious sort. But Count Marred is of the view that it's not so much a matter of good magic and evil, and more one of intention. You have been lucky, Seth. But you have also been very brave. And, of course, completely foolish. Those two things often go hand in hand.'

Seth couldn't think of anything to say. He kept holding his mother's hand, hoping for a repeat of that returned pressure.

'I suppose congratulations are in order,' went on Pewter. 'This means you are now at the start of absolutely the most dangerous and difficult path you could ever possibly wish to take. But it seems you have made your choice, Seth. I can only wish you the very best of luck! And I suppose it is down to me to say officially: welcome to the Elysee.'

'I passed my Prospect?' Seth stammered.

He had been so convinced all the choices and misjudgements he had made would mean he would never be welcomed into the magical world. It was going to take a while for the unbelievable news to sink in.

Then he felt again that rush of excitement he'd experienced when Calamus had told him he had incredible power within him. He might now get a chance to explore it.

Would he finally be able to achieve his cherished dream of becoming a talented sorcerer? It seemed utterly amazing after everything that had happened. As he stroked the treasured library card, the hand that gripped his mother's felt a definite pressure. It seemed to be telling him now his magical journey had truly begun.

Acknowledgements

Firstly, for all the hard work, passion, imagination and attention to detail you always bring – a thank you to the whole of the fantastic crew at my publisher, Chicken House.

I am so grateful to everyone who had a part to play in publishing this book, from my first reader and editor, Rachel, to another beautiful cover illustration from the ever-amazing Matt Saunders.

I really appreciate all the thought and care that has gone into the third of the Seth Seppi mysteries. And for having such faith in Seth and his friends.

I owe huge thanks to the amazing Blair Partnership, especially Jo Hayes and Jordan Lees for all their great help and friendliness and sound advice.

Also, I am now lucky enough to thank all my publishers around the world for their enthusiasm and care in bringing Seth Seppi to so many readers worldwide. I have been delighted to see copies of *The Last Chance Hotel* and *The Bad Luck Lighthouse* in all their loveliness, in so many different languages.

I owe a huge debt of gratitude to booksellers, librarians, teachers, authors and enthusiastic book lovers in so many countries, who have helped find a readership for the Seth Seppi mysteries. In particular,

I could not have wished for better help and support from my local bookshop, Mostly Books. Sarah, your whole team is incredible.

Finally, I seem to disappear into my writing cave increasingly these days, so thanks to my hugely supportive friends and family: to Mum, Alex and Tim, all the Nicholls, especially Oliver for his careful reading, to the Simpsons, to Pam and Ed and the Thornton-Greets.

And to my husband, Mark. I really could do none of this without you. Writing feels like it should be a solitary effort, but in reality relies on a huge team and you are the one at the centre who makes it all possible.